IN THE FIRST EARLY DAYS

OF MY DEATH

IN THE FIRST EARLY DAYS
OF MY DEATH

CATHERINE HUNTER

EDITIONS

Cover design by Terry Gallagher/Doowah Design.
Photo of Catherine Hunter by Anne Marie Resta.
Printed and bound in Canada by AGMV Marquis.

We acknowledge the support of the Canada Council for the Arts and
the Manitoba Arts Council for our publishing program.

National Library of Canada Cataloguing in Publication

Hunter, Catherine, 1957–
    In the first early days of my death / Catherine Hunter.

ISBN 0-921833-87-3

    I. Title.

PS8565.U5783I5 2002   C813'.54   C2002-905846-5
PR9199.3.H8255I5 2002

Signature Editions, P.O. Box 206, RPO Corydon
Winnipeg, Manitoba, R3M 3S7

This book is dedicated to
Manuela Dias (1963-2001)
and
Harry Rintoul (1956-2002)

Their radiance lives on.

Author's Note
This is a work of fiction. Although some of the places resemble real locations, all of the characters are figments of the author's imagination. In no way are they intended to reflect any actual persons, either living or dead.

I am very grateful for assistance from the Manitoba Arts Council in the first early days of this project. My thanks to the editors of *Contemporary Verse Two* in which earlier incarnations of this work were excerpted under its working title, "Phantom Pain" (Vol. 21.1, Summer 1998 and Vol. 23.1, Summer 2000).

Thanks also to Anne Marie Resta for insightful reading and glimpses into the darkroom, and thanks to Antony (Ben) Benton for crack research assistance. Any mistakes are my own.

The less one thinks about the theory of the *I Ching*, the more soundly one sleeps.

—Carl Jung

I

DIFFICULTY AT THE BEGINNING

In the first early days of my death, I could easily rise above the earth, past the massive, crenulated tops of the elm trees, over the scent of honeysuckle, into the summer sky that was thick and soft as a dark bolt of cloth, stars pushing themselves through like bright needles.

I could see the narrow, muddy Seine trickling north and the wide, muddy Assiniboine flowing east, both of them emptying into the Red River. I could see the whole length of the Red, its gleaming black surface with the wake of the moon upon it like a curved path I could trace to the horizon. I saw every house I'd ever lived in and the orange cross above the hospital where I'd been born and where I now lay. I peered into the windows of buildings and learned to part the glass like curtains so that I could pass right through.

If I wanted to, I could reach anywhere, feel the whole world at once, full of water and white sand and polar ice, fish in the oceans, red peppers and basil and lilies with their folded petals closed, unbearably lush and delicate and quiet in the darkness. I could hear everything, each exhalation of the humid air breathing through the branches far below, each muted puncture of the sky as another star poked through.

Some nights, if I let the wind blow through me, I could hear the dead begin to speak.

It's true.

Their voices, low and insistent, rustled past me like the wings of flying birds, and sometimes they sang.

But I was not interested in them.

—

Maybe my life would have ended differently if I'd accepted Mrs. Kowalski's invitation to join her at that protest rally at City Hall. Mrs. Kowalski was a determined woman, the most persuasive of my mothers, but I'd said no. I had to clean the house that day. I had to prune the oregano before it encroached any further on the lettuce patch. And I definitely had to phone a locksmith. Besides, Mrs. Kowalski was always protesting something. The year I was thirteen, it was pesticides. The year I was fourteen, it was pornography. By the time I was fifteen, I'd gone to live on Langside Street with old Mrs. Lamb, who was far beyond the mothering age and certainly past protesting anything. But Mrs. Kowalski never gave up. That summer, she was against gambling. Or at least gambling downtown.

The City of Winnipeg had changed a lot of bylaws so that All-Am Development could tear down four square blocks of Winnipeg's remaining core and erect a luxury casino complex, complete with gourmet restaurants, fountains, skylights, and a glass tower with a green spire that would be the tallest structure ever built in the city. This plan angered a lot of people because of the historic buildings that would be destroyed, including the Walker Theatre, where Nellie McClung had staged the famous mock parliament in 1914 which debated the issue of granting the vote to men. It enraged others simply because the mayor pushed through the bylaws without consulting the public. And it incensed people like Mrs. Kowalski, who didn't believe in games of chance. She grounded me once for playing poker with the boy next door, although we were only playing for pennies. She was the strictest mother I ever had, and wouldn't listen to excuses. "Don't push your luck," she always said. Maybe she was right, considering the way everything turned out.

It was because of my husband that I had to phone the locksmith. As a husband, Alika was sweet but less than helpful. The ordinary objects of the world confounded him. He was mystified by road maps, childproof cigarette lighters, income tax forms. Often I watched, enthralled, as he attempted some household project, like the time he lay motionless on his back beneath the kitchen sink for half an hour, the wrench loose in his big hand, water dripping down his fine, brown neck, while he tried to figure out how the pipes worked.

I have to admit that I took erotic pleasure in the leisurely workings of his mind, longed to be swallowed by the dense, lustrous cloak of obscurity that enveloped him. His brown, hooded eyes, with their shining, opaque pupils, rendered me weak, and when he raised his eyebrows, the young skin on his forehead wrinkling in perplexity, I was completely at his mercy.

The first time I met Alika, he was standing in the children's section of the library, holding a dozen yellow slips of paper in his hand. It was story time, and I was reading *Sleeping Beauty* to the kids, but I saw him. I noticed the high curve of his cheekbones, the shining lock of hair, colour of a crow's wing, falling across his forehead, the odd, distracted smile, as if he knew me from somewhere but couldn't quite place me yet. I was aware of his dark eyes watching as I turned the pages, and finally, when Sleeping Beauty lived happily ever after, I looked up and smiled at him.

As the parents arrived to collect their children, Alika approached me, offering up the bouquet of yellow paper. He said he was looking for a book about perennials because he wanted to grow some in his backyard. He'd been searching through the computer, writing down the titles of books about gardening, and now he wanted to know how to find them. He had not written down the call numbers.

I guided him back to the computer and tried to explain the Dewey Decimal system. I copied a list of relevant numbers and placed it in his hand.

"The numbers on the books correspond to the numbers on the shelves," I told him.

"Right," he said, as if he had always known this and had somehow simply forgotten it. This apparent lapse did not disturb him in the least. He sat so passively, with such utter acceptance, that I wondered how he had ever conceived the notion of growing anything. How had he found his way down to the library?

I pointed him toward the non-fiction, saying, "Good luck with your garden." And then, on impulse, "Come by and let me know how it goes."

He smiled. I saw a sudden flicker, deep within the brown iris of his left eye, a brief flare, like the waver and fizzle of a dying lightbulb. He handed me a business card. Then he was gone. I learned later that his right eye was made of glass. Maybe that was what made him so compelling to me that first day, so attractively off-kilter. I stood in the library, holding the card he had given me, feeling it warm my hands.

"Wendy," the head librarian said. "Hey, Wen-dee. Come on back to earth."

His mother named him Alika, meaning "defender of humankind," because that was the name his Hawaiian grandmother suggested just before she died. Rosa and her husband had already chosen the name Michael for a boy, but when Alika was born, Rosa decided to respect her mother-in-law's wishes.

Rosa was lonely in Hawaii. She had only intended to stay there for a three-week vacation, but then she fell in love with Alika's father, and when her friends returned to Canada, she stayed behind. Shortly after they married, she discovered he travelled so much on business that she was often left alone. And so for company, she visited his parents. She grew close to them, caring for her mother-in-law during a long illness, and finally, holding her hand and praying with her as she passed away. Rosa's husband had been out of town when his mother died. He was busy building a tourist hotel in Waikiki, and so it fell to Rosa to console her devastated father-in-law, to arrange the funeral and cremation.

When Rosa went into labour a month later, her husband was back in Waikiki. She drove herself to the hospital, delivered and nursed and named the baby without him. The name Alika never really suited her son, not even when he was a baby, Rosa admitted, but it was bad luck to disobey the dead.

Rosa was inordinately superstitious. She believed in destiny, in omens and premonitions. But most of all she believed in bad luck. Anything could trigger it. The usual things, of course—black cats, stepladders, umbrellas that sprang open unexpectedly, by accident, inside the house. But she also knew other rules I'd never heard of, exotic rules, involving all manner of innocent tasks—the peeling of apples, the sweeping of floors. It was perilous, I learned from my mother-in-law, to pick up the telephone in the middle of a ring. Where, I wondered, did that one come from? I'd always considered superstitions to be ancient, like religions, but for Rosa, even the modern world was a labyrinth of chance, a game of snakes and ladders that required constant vigilance.

But Rosa never learned what had caused the worst luck of all. Although she wracked her conscience for evidence of a forgotten rite, some criminal recklessness involving salt or mirrors, she could never find a reason for the car accident that had nearly killed her children.

Alika and his sister, Noni, were small at the time, nine and ten years old. As usual, their father was away on a job. He was supervising a construction site in Honolulu, and would miss his father's birthday. So Rosa had dutifully driven the children across Maui to visit their widowed grandfather at his nursing home in Wailuku. At twilight, when visibility was at its worst, a weary long-distance truck driver, hauling a load of pineapples, wobbled and veered toward the white line in the middle of the highway. Rosa swerved toward the shoulder, and her car spun wildly. The truck hit Rosa's rear door, sending Noni's tender body sailing through the air. Noni lost her leg because of that crash. Alika lost his eye and part of his right ear. I sometimes wondered if he hadn't lost something else, too, something less tangible, a way of operating in the practical world.

Loving Alika was irresistible. But I sometimes worried that marrying him so quickly had been improvident. At first I considered his bewilderment to be a sort of courtship ritual, an act of seduction. I expected it to dissipate eventually. After all, he had a good job. He was a photographer at Gino's Portrait Studio, where he was apparently quite competent, even exemplary. So I supposed that a latent intelligence huddled somewhere within, that it would someday emerge into our life together. But after nearly a year of marriage, there was no sign of it.

The problem wasn't Alika's clumsiness with household objects, which I found endearing, even sexy. It wasn't his failure to read directions properly, navigate the library, put gas in the car, remember the grocery list or where he put his keys. All of this I could forgive, did forgive, every night, the moment he cuddled up beside me in bed. No, the worst of it was his stupidity when it came to people, especially women. Especially Evelyn James.

Where Evelyn was concerned, Alika was blind, deaf, and brain-dead. It was Evelyn, not incidentally, who was responsible for the perennials. She had suggested the idea to him when they were first dating. She wanted something permanent to commemorate their relationship.

According to Alika, there was never any hope of permanence with Evelyn. She was no more than a fling, a one-month stand. He'd met her at the corner convenience store, where she worked the evening shift, and asked her out—just on a whim. But it didn't last. She became possessive, made him claustrophobic. He began to slip away from her as soon as he met me, he said. As soon as he saw me at the library, he wanted me to be his wife. All romantics lie like that, though they don't even know they're doing it.

"What if I'd quit my job?" I asked him once. "What if you'd gone back to the library and I wasn't there?"

"I'd have found you," he said.

"You would have forgotten all about me."

"I'd have found you," he repeated, no more insistent than before, calmly convinced he was telling the truth.

"What if I'd moved away? Out of town?"

"You didn't," he said. He was puzzled. What was the point of this conversation?

Even I wasn't sure what the point was. I'd never been like that before, insecure, asking dumb, unanswerable questions, demanding proof of a love that was plainly audible in his voice. It was Evelyn who made me like that. It was Evelyn's fault that I felt uneasy, watchful. That I began to lose faith.

The last morning of my life began normally enough. I was on holidays, so I came downstairs in my pyjamas and made blueberry pancakes and coffee. Then I called Alika into the kitchen for breakfast. I handed him his coffee and he raised the cup to his lips.

"Sugar," I warned him.

"Thanks," he said. He put the cup back on the table and added sugar.

"I'm going to get dressed," I said. "I want to start on the garden early, before it gets too hot."

Upstairs, I showered and changed into shorts and a T-shirt. I started to make the bed, but when I picked up the pillows, I discovered, on Alika's side, a single nylon stocking, hidden underneath. I picked it up and drew it slowly between my fingers. I smelled it. I knew whose it was.

When we were first married, I rarely thought about Evelyn. She never crossed my mind, except for those odd moments when I'd encounter one or another of her belongings in Alika's house. He had told me that she used to spend every weekend at his place, and it was no wonder, I thought, that she'd misplaced a few things, given the state of his housekeeping. Alika's house had appalled me, the first time he invited me over. I found myself washing dishes, wiping the counter, mopping the floor. Alika didn't understand the importance of these details. He grew impatient, wanting me to sit down, drink a glass of wine, listen to music, talk to him. But I couldn't relax when the kitchen floor was so dirty that the beer cartons were glued to the linoleum.

"Come on, Wendy," he'd say. "Forget about the linoleum. There are more important things in life."

"This *is* life," I'd tell him.

In the fall, shortly after our wedding, I found a pair of Evelyn's earrings, a compact, and a silk scarf that still carried traces of her trademark scent—lavender, a strangely old-fashioned choice. It seemed as though Evelyn had slowly come unravelled, leaving a meandering trail of detritus in her wake. I pictured her as a slovenly, absent-minded girl, the kind with nubby sweaters, chewed fingernails, band-aids on her knee. I cleaned and tidied, claiming the house as my own. I removed every loose trace of Evelyn and forgot about her all winter.

But early in the spring, tucked behind a couch cushion, I found a signed photograph of my husband's former girlfriend. She looked about twenty-two, a few years younger than me. She was wearing a pink sundress and matching sandals. She didn't look like a convenience store clerk, at least not like any I'd ever seen. It wasn't that she was beautiful. She wasn't even very attractive, though her brushed hair emitted a faintly golden glow, reminiscent of honey, of peaches and butter. But she was focussed so intensely on the photographer that her image was rivetting. I studied her hopeful eyes, her hungry smile, and something tugged at me, deep within my belly. I didn't mention the photo to Alika. I kept it in a drawer for a couple of days before I threw it away. But that photograph was only the beginning. It seemed that the flotsam and jetsam of Evelyn had resurfaced. All summer long, I found more of her belongings scattered throughout the house—a jewelled comb, a little monogrammed notebook, blank inside—yes, I looked, I rifled the pages. By that point, I was worried. And then I found the stocking under Alika's pillow.

I sat on the bed for a while with the stocking in my hand, alarmed by its sheerness, its silky texture and unmistakable lavender scent. I considered the possibility that it had lain unnoticed in our laundry hamper for twelve months, found its way accidentally into a recent load of wash and, in the dryer, become stuck by static electricity to this pillow case. It didn't seem likely. Not in this humidity. When Alika finished his pancakes and came upstairs, I presented him with the stocking.

"What's this?" he asked.

"What do you think it is? It's a woman's stocking. Evelyn's stocking. Do you want to tell me how it got under your pillow?"

Alika looked at me. He picked up the pillow and looked underneath, then fluffed it and tossed it aside. "Under there?"

"Under there. And I changed the sheets yesterday morning, so how did it get there?"

"I don't know," he said.

"Alika," I said. "Has Evelyn been here? Was she here yesterday? Just tell me."

"I don't know."

"How could you not know?"

"I didn't see her," he offered.

I sighed. "Did you forget to lock the door yesterday?"

"You know I always lock the door," he said.

"How could she get in without you seeing her, then, if the door was locked?"

He was quiet for a minute. Then he said, "Maybe she unlocked it?"

"Alika! She has a key to the house?"

"Well, of course she has a key," he said. "She practically lived here last summer."

"For God's sake," I said. But I knew there was no point explaining to him how foolish he was, so I just said, "I'm getting the locks changed. Today."

Alika lay down on top of the bedspread and rested his cheek on the sheet where Evelyn's stocking had been lying less than ten minutes ago. I shuddered.

"It was in our *bed*," I groaned.

Alika turned and looked at me studiously, as if he'd finally decided to take this issue seriously.

"But how did it get there?" he asked.

I scrutinized his expression. Nothing but the same blank density he offered to the water pipes. He seemed genuinely, maddeningly, nonplussed.

That was when Mrs. Kowalski called and invited me to the protest rally. I talked to her on the phone for a while, listening to her concerns about the city and giving her excuses why I couldn't go. When I hung up, I felt a little guilty about not helping her out. So I suggested to Alika that he go downtown and shoot some pictures of the event. Sometimes he made a little extra money by selling local photos to *Uptown Magazine.*

I also wanted him out of the way so I could phone his sister Noni. I needed to talk to someone who could think clearly.

Noni wore a pink plastic prosthesis which she strapped to her thigh with a complicated leather harness. It was uncomfortable, and she frequently removed it in the privacy of her own home, or in ours. That last afternoon, as she listened to my tale of Evelyn's stocking, Noni sat on my back porch, her chin in her hands, shaking her head in disbelief. I was pulling beets and swatting at mosquitoes. It was hot, and my bare legs were streaked with sweat and dirt. Noni lifted up her cotton skirt and untangled the harness. She leaned the leg, with its little pink foot in its pink running shoe, against the wooden steps.

"Are you all right?" I asked her. Noni's amputated leg still hurt her sometimes, even though it wasn't there. Her doctor claimed this was perfectly normal. The nerves were gone, but the receptors in the brain were still alive and waiting, like telephone receivers, for messages. Sometimes they became confused and thought they were hearing from that long-lost leg. The doctor called this "phantom pain." It wasn't dangerous, he said. He recommended Aspirin, and Noni took two, extra-strength, when the invisible leg began to ache. But there was nothing else she could do about it. There was no known cure for phantom pain.

"I'm fine," she said. "But you're going to get heatstroke." She poured two glasses of lemonade and told me to sit down for a minute.

I laid the beets down on the porch in the shade and picked up the glass of lemonade, listening to the ice cubes clink and fizz. I held the glass against my damp neck. Then I drank it down and poured myself another.

We sat in silence, surveying the garden.

"Do you think she's dangerous?" Noni asked.

I looked at the flaming yellow poppies, the tall zinnias stuffed to bursting with surreal orange and russet petals, the cabbages fat as green planets, and the nicotiana flowers bending over them like white stars. Everything had grown too large, too quickly, that summer. The morning glory had topped the fence early in July, climbed across the rough shingles of the tool shed walls and up the telephone pole, where it bloomed a bright continuous blue against the sky. The yellow beans were plump and ready to be picked, their stalks out of control, strangling each other. Great bushes of crackerjack marigolds exploded among the tomato plants. It was only the twenty-first of August, but the pumpkins were already round and symmetrical as beach balls, and the zucchini were so numerous I had taken to leaving them on neighbours' doorsteps, like abandoned babies, in the middle of the night.

"I don't know," I said. I got up and returned to the beet patch, thinking about Evelyn. Of course she was dangerous, in an obvious way. She was interfering with my marriage, disturbing my peace of mind, making me crazy. But that's not what Noni meant, and we both knew it. Noni meant, was she violent? Was she likely to throw rocks through the window, threatening notes attached? Would she show up at the library, a pipe bomb in her backpack? Slit her wrists in my bathtub one day, so that I'd come home to find bloody water trickling under the door, seeping into the hall carpet?

"What can I do, anyway, even if she is dangerous?" I asked. I braced myself in the mud, struggling to pull up a particularly fat beet.

"There has to be some way to get rid of her," Noni said.

"How?"

"There has to be a way," she said.

But before we could formulate any sort of plan, we were interrupted.

A fat little chow chow came streaking through my open back gate and tore right through the garden, with no regard for the vegetables and flowers.

Noni, who was afraid of dogs, grabbed for her leg and scrambled to tie the harness to her thigh.

"Hey!" I shouted. But the dog paid no attention. It trampled the romaine lettuce and raced straight through the oregano, trailing a red leash from its collar.

A moment later, the dog was followed by a burly red-faced man, who was a little more careful about the garden. He rushed down the path, then stopped when he saw me.

"Pardon us," he said. He was panting slightly. "My dog seems to have taken a liking to your cat." He gestured toward the elm tree, where the dog sat expectantly, waggling its rear end. Its ears were rigid, its nose pointing toward the sky.

I looked up and saw a yellow cat sitting calmly on a low branch. "That's not my cat," I said.

He approached his dog from the side and slid his hand into the handle of the leash. "Sorry to disturb you," he said. "Poppy is a little, ah, undisciplined."

"I see that," I said. I looked at the crushed, muddy leaves of the romaine. "What a mess."

"Sorry," he said again. He seemed mortified.

He was surprisingly timid for his size. He must have been six-foot-four, with thick, powerful arms, and a bit of a beer belly. He was in his early forties, I guessed, but his face was as freckled and sheepish as a little boy's. He was sweating profusely, and I wondered why he was wearing a suit jacket on such a humid day. Then I recognized him.

"Say, you're that cop, aren't you? I mean, aren't you the police officer? In that brick house with all the trees?"

"That's right. Felix Delano. I'm a police detective."

"I'm Wendy," I said. "Wendy Li. And this is my sister-in-law, Noni Li."

Noni had recovered her composure, but she stayed on the porch, away from Poppy.

"Li?" Felix asked. He looked with interest at Noni. "That's a Chinese name, isn't it?" He peered through the shadows of the porch, trying to see her face more clearly.

Noni didn't answer. She had no patience for that particular question, which she'd heard too often.

I'd carried the name for a year, but nobody ever asked me if it was Chinese. They just misspelled it, *Lee*, and I constantly had to correct them. This didn't bother me one bit. I loved being a Li. I had belonged to a lot of different families in my life, but the Li family was the only one I'd had a say in choosing.

"Do you want some lemonade?" I asked Felix.

He coughed, a little embarrassed by Noni's silence. "Sure," he said. "Thanks." Then he offered me his hand to shake, and I took it. His grip was strong, and he held on for a long moment, even though my fingers were caked with dirt.

After Felix left, with a bag of zucchini and broken romaine, I walked Noni out to her car, and we stood for a while, talking. We hadn't quite finished with the subject of Evelyn.

"She's probably harmless," I said. I was in a better mood by then. Felix had cheered me up. It made me feel a little safer to know I was friends—well, friendly—with a detective.

"Do you think so?" Noni asked.

"Probably," I said. "And anyway I'm getting the locks changed today." I looked at my watch. Where was that locksmith?

"I don't know," said Noni, as she got into her car. "I have a bad feeling about her."

"A premonition?"

Noni blushed. "Not exactly." Then she shivered suddenly, though it was still a sweltering day.

"What is it?" I asked.

"Oh, nothing," she said. "Don't pay any attention to me." She waved as she drove away.

I couldn't dismiss Noni's bad feeling so easily. And I didn't like that shiver. But I tried to reassure myself by remembering that Noni wasn't the clairvoyant in the family.

According to family legend, it was only Rosa who possessed the power of second sight. Rosa could often predict disasters. She'd had ominous intimations just before the Challenger spaceship exploded, before Mount St. Helens erupted, before the assassination of John Lennon. These powers manifested themselves shortly after her marriage. Alika's father was booked on a flight from Maui to Molokai, on one of those tiny, dangerous planes that belong to small, disreputable airlines. Rosa had a feeling about this, a sinister feeling. She begged him not to go, and finally, he relented—not that he believed in premonitions. He thought she was making it up because she wanted him to stay home. In any case, the plane crashed, spectacularly. For no apparent reason, the fuselage cracked in two, right down the middle—a stress fracture, they called it later—and the tiny aircraft burst into flames, went down and sank beneath the Pacific waves. Noni's eyes had been dark and wide and serious when she told me this tale. Her mother had a gift, she said.

Why, then, I wondered, had they had that terrible car accident? Why had Rosa not seen, or felt, the truck approaching on the highway, not sensed the sleepiness of the driver? Why had she not been warned that her children would be traumatized, disfigured? That she would suffer that unspeakable fear, searching for her daughter in the ditch by the dark side of the road, finding her with her knee torn and twisted in that impossible way?

Alika had not been thrown from the car. He remained in the front seat, where metal and glass flew at his face like shrapnel from an explosion, piercing his shoulder and neck, breaking his jaw, perforating his right eye and destroying it completely.

You'd think a mother, a psychic mother, could have seen that coming.

The locksmith was supposed to come at three, but at six o'clock, he still had not arrived. Alika came home from City Hall, and we ate gelati for dinner and smoked a couple of cigarettes, but he didn't stay long. He had to work the late shift at the portrait studio. There was a backlog of orders for graduation and wedding prints, and Gino wanted Alika to process them all by the weekend.

"How was the rally?" I asked.

"Hot," he said. "But a huge crowd turned up. Mrs. Kowalski was happy."

"Get some good pictures?"

"I think so. The light was fabulous, and I used Gino's zoom lens." He took his camera out of his bag and laid it on the kitchen table. "I'll develop these tomorrow," he said. "Right now, I'd better go."

"How late do you think you'll be?"

"Late," he said. "Don't wait up." He kissed the top of my head and left.

I put the ice-cream bowls in the sink and walked to the window to watch Alika drive away. He was sitting in his car at the curb, waiting for me to appear. I waved. Alika started the engine and drove down the street without even looking at the road, smiling and waving to me out the window. I didn't know it was the last time I would ever see him like that, so confident in his own luck.

I spent the evening cleaning. First I washed all the windows with vinegar and newspaper. Then I dusted and vacuumed the entire house. Next, I took Alika's camera up to his darkroom. I hoped he'd taken some good shots of the protest at City Hall, shots he could sell. Sometimes his photographs seemed to miss the point. He'd covered a friend's wedding last autumn and come away with more shots of the trees outside the church than of the people. A pile of these pictures lay scattered on his counter, a series of close-ups in which all you could see were two brittle veins of a yellow, translucent leaf. They were beautiful, but you couldn't even tell what they were unless he told you. I stacked them neatly and set them aside. I couldn't do anything about the rest of the mess in the darkroom. It was full of equipment I couldn't put away because I didn't know what it was. I just cleared a space on the counter, so I could leave the camera in plain sight, where he could find it, and closed the door on the chaos.

I got the silver polish from the upstairs closet, and a few soft rags. I went back into the bedroom and took out the photo of Alika's family so that I could clean the silver picture frame. The photo had been taken a few short months before the unlucky car crash, and Alika was small and unscarred, sitting high on his father's shoulders. I often studied the face of Alika's father, who I knew only through his infrequent letters. I'd never met him. Even Alika barely knew him.

The car crash had broken the family apart, extinguishing a marriage that was already growing cold. Rosa had become increasingly self-sufficient during her husband's long absences, but his failure to stand by her side while Alika and Noni were in hospital was the final straw. As soon as the children were well enough to travel,

Rosa had brought them to Winnipeg to visit her parents. And, with their financial help, she'd stayed in the city ever since.

She had rarely taken her children to visit their father in Hawaii, and their father never came to Canada—he'd developed a fear of flying—so Alika and Noni had known him mainly through cards and letters, telephone calls and birthday presents. But as I knew very well, those things were much, much better than nothing.

I polished the frame and replaced the photograph. Then I laid out my silver brush and mirror and my silver music box, which had been a Christmas present from my mother Mrs. Keller. I kept a number of small, personal items in this music box. Nothing valuable, really. Unless you wanted to count the letter from my birth mother.

Mrs. Hill, my social worker, had given the letter to me when she retired. I was about twelve then, and fascinated by my mother's handwriting, sometimes tracing over the letters with my fingers, making the same curves and loops that she had made so long ago. The letter was written on two pages of foolscap in ballpoint pen. It was double-spaced and single-sided. You'd think she could easily have crammed in a few more words, but no. She came to the end of the second page and just stopped, signing the letter, *love, Your Mother.*

The letter was mainly about my father, how handsome he was, etc. Unfortunately, however, "circumstances prevented" their marrying at the time, by which I understood, when I grew to be older, that he was married to somebody else. My mother had been too young to raise me on my own. But she'd had great hopes. She and my father would eventually be united. Then she would come for me. We would all be together.

That was why I had so many foster parents—because my mother believed for too long in the eventual triumph of romance. By the time she finally let me go, signed the papers and made me eligible for legal adoption, I was nearly four years old. Too big. Nobody wanted me for keeps.

My father, the letter said, was my mother's heart, her life. "You were not the product of some casual fling," my mother wrote. "You were born of my first, my last, my most precious love. It is very important to me that you understand that."

I understood, all right. I got the picture. A great drama had surrounded my conception and birth. A grand, greedy, voluptuous, star-crossed passion had occurred, and I had been left out of it.

I was the residue.

After I polished the music box, I planned to tackle the silver in the kitchen. We didn't have much—just the cake knife from our wedding, a tea tray, and half a dozen teaspoons. All of it was tarnished, tinged with a milky blue, and I wanted to make it gleam again. But first I decided to take another shower. I was sweaty from gardening and doing housework in the heat wave. My clothing stuck to me as I peeled it off. I walked naked to the bathroom, turned on the tap, and stepped into the tub. Then I heard a knock on the door. The locksmith, I thought. Wouldn't you know it? I dried myself as quickly as I could. The knocking didn't let up.

"Hold on," I muttered. The knocking continued. Then I heard the front door open. Alika, despite his promises, had forgotten to lock it. I stepped out into the hall, intending to grab some clothing from the bedroom. But when I heard footsteps coming up the stairs, I panicked. I dived naked into the hall closet and closed the door.

The footsteps came up the stairs rapidly and lightly— a small person, I thought. Probably a woman. Evelyn! Of course. She had let herself in with her key. Noni's question about Evelyn raced through my mind: "Do you think she's dangerous?" I wasn't about to find out, especially with me naked and her fully clothed. I heard the footsteps enter the bedroom, drawers opening and closing, a rustling sound. Then a feeble, dramatic sigh. She's obsessed with Alika, I thought. She's stalking him. She has—what was it called? Erotomania.

The footsteps left the bedroom, and I trembled a little as they approached the closet where I hid, but they passed on by, and I heard the door to Alika's darkroom open. Then there was silence for a long time. Too long.

There was no room in that closet. It was stuffed full of things we didn't need at the moment, like winter jackets, and things I couldn't bear to part with, like the lace veil I'd worn at my wedding last fall, and the butterfly kite I'd made with the kids at the library in the spring. We'd taken that kite out during a strong wind, and on its maiden flight it smashed into a tree and broke its frame, tearing one of its wings and losing its string. Alika said he was going to fix it, but he never got around to it. So it sat in the linen closet, along with all the other junk, preventing me from moving. My legs were filling up with pins and needles. The muscles in my calves began to cramp. I shifted my weight an inch, and the buckle of an old snowshoe bit into my bare heel.

I took a chance. I pulled a parka off the hook inside the closet and put it on. I reached for the doorknob and, as quietly as possible, I turned it.

—

I have never remembered opening that door. All I knew was that later in the evening, as I wandered the empty rooms of my house, I felt strangely detached. My head hurt, and I couldn't seem to get anything done. I'd planned to finish the housework and make a borscht from the beets, then maybe bake a special treat for tomorrow's dessert. I saw the cookbook lying open on the table to the recipe for chocolate kiwi pie. I felt a brief pang of hunger when I looked at the photograph, but I didn't do anything about it. I didn't even begin to tidy up the kitchen. The tarnished silver sat out on the counter, waiting to be cleaned. The breakfast dishes and the ice-cream bowls floated listlessly in the sink, the soap bubbles long since gone flat, the water cold. My sense of purpose had left me entirely.

I drifted into the living room and watched out the window for Alika to come home. There was something important I had to tell him, but I couldn't remember what it was, exactly. The shadows were lengthening across all the lawns in the neighbourhood. The sun had beaten down ferociously all day, shrivelling the roots of the plants. I thought that I really should water the garden. But I couldn't seem to leave the house. The sky darkened and a fat moon came up. After a while I could hear thunder rumbling across the prairie toward the city and then the lightning started and finally the cool, hard rain beat down. I knew I should close the window, I should close all the windows in the house, but instead I stayed there watching as the rain turned into hail, trying to understand what was happening to me.

2

DARKENING OF THE LIGHT

Evelyn James woke up with the unsettling knowledge that she was not alone. For years now, she'd been haunted by her twin brother, Mark, who was killed on a trestle bridge at the age of thirteen when he tried to outrace a freight train on his bicycle, and sometimes he'd appear outside her window at dawn, usually wearing his black and red magic cape, waving his fifty-cent magic wand in long swoops as if writing words in the air, some message Evelyn couldn't decipher. But this wasn't Mark. This was a thin white streak, a flickering presence that could barely sustain itself.

She tried her usual cure for insomnia, reciting in her mind long lists of the most monotonous things she could imagine, like the rows of overpriced canned goods at the convenience store: condensed milk, devilled ham, kidney beans, creamed corn. But it wasn't working. For some reason, her thoughts kept turning compulsively toward the garden in the backyard of the house that should have been hers. The pink roses that bloomed where her own had withered and died. She tried listing the names of the plants she had seen when she passed by: marigolds, zinnias, snow peas, leafy potato plants in straight, weeded rows, and cabbages, their outer leaves so wide and delicately thin it seemed they might flap their green wings and fly away.

Ever since that woman had moved into Alika's house, the ground had shifted, the earth had opened up and turned over, revealing a dark, fertile loam beneath its surface. Evelyn had dug out there herself, dug until her back nearly cracked in two, and she knew the soil was marbled through with clay like streaks of fat in a cheap pot roast.

But that woman had dug and the yard had yielded up its vitamins, surrendered itself with plump tomatoes and waxy yellow peppers, bumblebees and butterflies and poppies and even carnations—carnations! In Manitoba! And early this spring, the bulbs—dark, purple tulips and crocuses—no, this was not going to put her to sleep. It only made her angry.

She turned over and pulled the chain of her bedside lamp. In the darkness, she tried again. The jars this time: horseradish, mustard, mayonnaise, jam…

—

Felix Delano lay in bed with his wife, Alice, and his chow chow, Poppy. He was trying to wake his wife up slowly, beginning with her feet. He slid his calloused heel across her slim arches, across her ankles, hoping to tickle her. The dog woke up and looked at him, but Alice did not stir. Alice lay facing her husband, her mouth half open as if she were about to say something in a dream. Felix slid his foot up over her calf and wrapped his arm around her waist. He blew into the hollow of her throat. The dog whimpered softly and hopped off the bed. Alice smiled, but she was still asleep. Felix began to stroke her hair. He spoke into her ear. He named the things he would make her for breakfast if she would wake up.

Alice had always loved to sleep. But lately she threw herself into it with such great pleasure that Felix wondered if she were trying to avoid him. Every evening, early, she'd wriggle under the covers and snuffle into the pillow like a burrowing animal. Then she'd lie motionless for nine or ten hours. This morning, she was engaged in a particularly dedicated slumber. Felix gave up. He swung his legs out onto the floor and stood. Poppy followed him into the kitchen.

It was August twenty-second. The heat wave had been broken by the storm the night before, and the birds were chirping. Felix tried to focus on the day ahead, tried to put his wife's sleeping body out of his mind. He opened all the windows, letting in sunlight and air and the undulating whisper of thousands of delicate poplar leaves rising and falling with the morning breeze. He put the kettle on and walked to the front door to retrieve the newspaper. The whole street looked clean and quiet, relieved of the oppressive heat that, for weeks, had woken everyone at sunrise. He carried the paper back to the kitchen and spread it open on the table. On the front page, below the fold, the mayor's face looked up at him, smiling.

Felix had seen the mayor yesterday, trying to evade the protesters at City Hall, and he wanted to read about the rally. But first he glanced at the top story, illustrated by the photo of a smiling man in a white coat, the city entomologist. The mosquito count was levelling off due to the lack of rain. The entomologist announced that the worst of the plague was over. Felix smiled grimly, thinking of the rain water that had collected overnight in bird baths, ditches, old rubber boots and pails that people left out in their yards. Since yesterday, the city had become one gigantic mosquito breeding ground. He turned his attention to the story with the big picture of Mayor Douglas. The mayor was shaking hands with a large bald man in a dark suit, but the men were not looking at each other. They were beaming at the camera in a celebratory way.

The caption identified the bald man as the president of All-Am Corporation. According to the story, All-Am was ready to go ahead with the new casino complex that would revitalize downtown Winnipeg. The old buildings were already empty and ready for the wrecking ball. One brief paragraph mentioned that a citizens' group had persuaded a judge to sign an order preventing the demolition until they could make a presentation at a public forum. But the reporter implied that the citizens' group was a small fringe element, the order an insignificant hitch, a temporary delay. Felix read the article twice, but he saw no mention of yesterday's rally. Typical journalism. The reporter had probably spent the day at the beach.

Felix made his tea and carried it out to the screened porch. He sat on the couch and set his cup on the wicker table, next to the *Book of Changes*, which was lying open where he'd left it yesterday morning. The three coins in their jade box gleamed in the sunlight.

He held the box in both hands for a moment, contemplating the intricate morning shadows cast by the porch lattice and the poplar trees, the small slivers and crosses of sunlight that mottled the walls and wooden floor of the porch. A slight breeze came up, and the branches moved; the pattern shifted. He rattled the jade box gently and opened his hands, letting the coins fall through the air.

—

The mayor's office was on the sixth floor of City Hall. Not high enough for the mayor when he was in one of the majestic, proprietary moods that seized him unexpectedly from time to time. When such a mood came upon him, as it did this morning, he would saunter briskly down the corridors, descend to the basement, and follow the underground paths that snaked beneath Portage and Main until he was directly under the Commodity Exchange Building. Then he'd enter the elevator and rise to the thirty-third floor, where he'd pretend to require a consultation with the accountants of his construction firm—his former firm, that is—he'd had to sign it over to a blind trust when he was elected. Today, the accountants were not yet in their offices. It was far too early. The mayor nodded to the security guards, then used his key to let himself into the empty suite. He stood alone before the magnificent bank of windows that ran the entire circumference of the building. He savoured these moments, his whole city spread out below him like the toy towns he used to build as a child. He felt he could reach down and pluck up a tree, or a whole forest of trees, move a church or two, a department store. Maybe push the whole North End of the city a little farther north.

He smiled as his eyes passed over the site of the future casino. The publicity in today's paper was good, and it would only get better, thanks to his wife, Louise. He glanced at his watch. Where *was* Louise? She'd promised to call him after her morning jog through Assiniboine Park. She was on a fitness craze these days, and kept up her daily exercise religiously, despite the vicious heat, and despite the fact that she didn't seem to be losing any weight.

—

Noni's leg ached more than usual this morning. She wondered if her lost knee was developing arthritis. Stiffly, she sat up in bed and grabbed the crutch beside the dresser. Then she swung herself down the hall of her apartment and into the kitchen, where she prepared a breakfast of coffee and Aspirins.

She'd dreamed last night that she was flying a kite in Happyland Park, with Wendy. It was Wendy's red butterfly kite, the one that, in reality, had a crack in its frame and a broken string. In the dream, the crack had healed, and instead of a string, the kite was attached to a red dog leash, and Wendy was running across the grass beside the stream, trying to launch the kite into the air.

"Wait up!" Noni called, but Wendy ran farther and farther away, toward the little fork where the stream entered the Seine River. Noni couldn't keep up. Soon, all she could see was the kite ascending above the trees. It fluttered its way along the banks of the Seine, north, toward the Red. And then she'd woken with her knee on fire.

Noni rubbed her eyes, trying to clear away the wisps of the dream that lingered in her mind's eye. She had work to do. The pattern for a customer's new dress lay spread on the sewing table in her living room, still pinned to its tangerine silk, and the woman was coming tomorrow for a fitting. Noni would have finished the dress yesterday if Wendy hadn't called. She could have begged off, saying she was too busy. But Wendy, usually carefree and casual, had sounded worried, so Noni had gone. Not that she'd been much help, she reflected. She'd intended to set Wendy's mind at ease, but the story about the stocking had been sinister. How in the world could Evelyn's stocking end up under Alika's pillow? Noni couldn't think of any but the most obvious answer.

She gulped another Aspirin. She had to control the pain if she was going to accomplish anything today. She had to finish that dress and then start on the growing pile of mending and alterations. And she needed supplies. She glanced at the clock. The sewing shop wasn't open yet, but she could start a list. She needed pins, orange thread, two bobbins…

The telephone rang. Noni waited for the ring to come to a full stop, so she could pick up the receiver with no danger of bad luck. As she waited, a vague image of her brother began to form in her mind, but Alika didn't seem like his usual self at all. There was something odd about the image, something contorted, as if he, too, was suffering.

—

Felix knew his peaceful morning was too good to last. Just as he tossed the coins for the third time, he heard the telephone ring. It was his partner, Paul, alerting him to an emergency right there on Felix's own street.

Minutes later, Paul briefed Felix as they drove one short block down St. Catherine. "Caucasian female. Unconscious. They're trying to revive her." He pulled up in front of a white frame house. The street pulsed with the flashing lights of a rescue unit.

Inquisitive neighbours had gathered on the boulevard. One lady, still in her nightgown, stood on the sidewalk, peering with blatant curiosity into the open door. Felix pushed her aside, and suddenly he recognized the white picket fence, the morning glory, the lilac bush. He ran ahead of Paul into the house.

In the front hall, at the bottom of the stairs, two paramedics worked frantically over a small figure on the floor. A young officer crouched in the entry to the living room, watching. She recognized Felix and straightened up.

"Detective Delano," she said.

"Who found her?"

"The husband. Came home and found her lying right there." She pointed. "Says he didn't move her."

Felix nodded. "What else?"

"Well, it's weird. Lady's wearing nothing but a parka. Looks like she fell down the stairs. I don't see how. There's no smell of booze. Christ, she's young. I don't know."

"Anyone else here?" Felix asked. "Other family?"

"The husband's sister's here. They're in the kitchen."

"I'll go talk to them," Paul said.

Felix circled the medics, staying well out of their way as they worked. One of them pounded the woman's bare chest with a force that threatened to shatter her rib-cage. Felix stood as close as he dared and scanned the body for signs of violence. All he could see was a thick lock of pale brown hair, matted with blood, and a sunburned cheek, incongruous against the fur of the parka hood. He looked at the face. Yes. It was Wendy Li. The girl from the garden.

——

It was like one of those nightmares, those recurring dreams in which I was never prepared. In which I was lost or had lost something essential—my clothing or, worse, a puppy or an infant that was in my care.

At first, all I could think of were the dirty dishes in the sink, the fact that I hadn't made any pie, that we were out of coffee, and the house was full of people. What would they think? Noni was there, and our neighbour, Felix the cop from down the street, and a pile of strangers, and here we were with nothing to offer them. There was some kind of project going on in the hall, something urgent that I knew I should have been involved in. Everyone was expecting me to participate, but I couldn't remember how. I tried to concentrate on what they were saying, but there were other voices, calling from some other place as well, and my consciousness stretched thin as cheesecloth, a torn and threadbare sheet through which I wavered, glimpsing the scene in hazy, disconnected images.

Then, in a moment of clarity, I saw myself lying there, naked in a crowd of strangers. So I relaxed. I was obviously dreaming, after all.

—

On the evening of their eleventh birthday, Evelyn James and her brother Mark went swimming at Happyland Park. They were giddy and full of birthday cake, not caring that the sky was overcast and the air was cool. Mark shivered uncontrollably by the side of the pool, drops of chlorinated water dappling his thin shoulders, his lips bright blue. "Are you cold?" she asked him, and he dropped to his knees on the hard tiles, suffered his first seizure, fell unconscious into the deep end.

Sometimes, the spirit of Mark appeared to Evelyn wearing a bathing suit, as if Mark had become confused and thought he died by drowning. But he hadn't died that day at Happyland. The lifeguard pulled him out and called an ambulance. At the hospital, the doctors took Mark away, and Evelyn sat in the waiting room until her parents arrived.

She ran to them, crying, throwing her arms around both of them at once, but they peeled her gently away from their bodies and told her to wait. It was daylight by the time they remembered her. They came to the waiting room and sent her in a taxi to a neighbour's house. They stayed with Mark for three days while he had a lot of medical tests. That was how they found out about the tumour in his brain.

As it grew, Mark's tumour caused all kinds of strange behaviour, like roller skating off the teeter-totter, or trying to parachute, with a beach towel, from the highest limb of the crabapple tree. Or racing freight trains. Evelyn and her family had always believed this final, foolhardy act was another symptom of his dementia, but now that Evelyn was older, she wondered if it wasn't simply suicide.

Evelyn hoped that the tumour wasn't a genetic thing, like the blonde hair and the brown eyes she shared with Mark. Sometimes she thought she could feel it growing there, small and gelatinous, on the left side of her skull, behind her ear. Her left ear rang sometimes, a high sound, like a tinny sleigh bell, and sometimes she saw things that weren't really there.

Like this morning, just before the sun came up, that pale, uncertain smudge of light outside the window. A hallucination or a dream.

—

High in the Commodity Exchange Tower, the mayor thought of his wife with tenderness. This past year, Louise seemed to be emerging from the ennui that had enveloped her since the boys had grown up and moved away. She was taking an interest in the mayor's work again, in his city, and even, it seemed, in the mayor himself. Louise used to complain that Winnipeg was a hick town, but these days, she was enthusiastic about its future. A five-star, top-of-the-line casino would put Winnipeg on the map, she predicted, turn it into a tourist mecca. Especially with the exchange rates being what they were. Winnipeg would become famous and Mayor Douglas would be a celebrity.

Louise had even helped to facilitate the deal. When All-Am first proposed the development, City Council had hesitated. It was Louise who carefully researched the corporation's history and reported that they were reputable. It was Louise who discovered the loophole in the Historical Preservation Act that would allow them to demolish the Walker Theatre. And it was Louise, or rather, Louise's friendship with the newspaper's chief editor, that was responsible for the positive press the project was receiving now. The mayor's councillors were all—or almost all—convinced that the public wanted the casino, and a good majority of them had voted to provide All-Am with the forgivable loans and tax relief they needed to complete the project. The mayor hoped Louise could persuade her editor friend to give them even better press now. Their PR *had* to get better, if the mayor was going to beat that ragtag band of protesters with their rhetoric about history and their damned injunction against the demolition. Somehow, he had to get that order rescinded. That was the only thing All-Am was waiting for now. As soon as the judge lifted the injunction, All-Am would light the fuse, detonate the dirty old Walker, and history would be history.

The mayor strode across the reception area, entered the empty boardroom on the east side of the building, and surveyed the Forks, where the rivers met. He had heard this land was once an Aboriginal graveyard, but he didn't believe it. In any case, it was a shopping mall now, with a blue steel tower. It reminded the mayor of the plastic turrets of the toy castle that had been his childhood favourite. He had long wanted to expand this mall, but the area had unfortunate limitations. It was bounded on two sides by important downtown businesses, and on the other two sides by the banks of the Red and the Assiniboine. The mayor sighed. If only it were feasible to reroute the rivers.

—

As the paramedics continued to work over the body of Wendy Li, Felix tried to interview her family. Alika sat slumped in a kitchen chair, elbows on his knees and head in his hands, silent. His sister, the young woman Felix had met yesterday in the garden, was hovering over her brother, caressing his bent shoulders and cooing phrases that sounded like French to Felix.

Felix began with preliminaries, their names and addresses, dates of birth. Each time he posed a question, Noni answered for them both.

"And you were born—where?"

"Lahaina."

"China?"

"Hawaii. We're Canadian citizens now."

"I see," said Felix. "And, ah, your occupation?"

"I have my own business—I'm a seamstress," Noni said. "Alika's a photographer."

Felix pointed at Alika. "Doesn't he speak English?"

"Oh yes," she said.

"But you were speaking to him just now in—what?"

"French," Noni said softly.

"I see," said Felix, again. He didn't. But in light of Noni's confrontational stare, he thought he'd steer away from the subject of their origins. "So, ah, you came here this morning because your brother called you?"

"Yes."

"What exactly did he tell you on the phone?"

"He said he worked all night and when he came home, Wendy was lying at the bottom of the stairs. He couldn't rouse her, so he called me for help. I told him to phone an ambulance."

"He called you before he called 911?"

"Well, yes," said Noni. "He was distraught."

Felix found this suspicious. "Why didn't you call an ambulance immediately, Mr. Li?"

Alika merely moaned.

There was an ominous silence in the front hall. Felix rose to investigate. He saw the paramedics still crouched low beside Wendy. They had placed an oxygen mask over her face and were lifting her onto a stretcher.

"What's happening?" Felix asked.

"We've got a pulse," the medic said. "We're taking her in." She closed the parka over Wendy's naked breasts. She brushed a lock of hair from her forehead, and Felix remembered how Wendy had made this gesture herself, just yesterday, smearing a streak of grey mud across her hairline, into her eyebrows.

———

Finally, Evelyn gave up on sleep. She slid from her bed and performed her morning rituals, showering quickly and blow-drying her hair. Then she sat at the chair in front of her dresser and looked at the framed photograph she kept beside her bed while she brushed her hair. She was disciplined in her rituals, one hundred strokes every morning and the repetition of the spell.

"I travel beneath the earth to the pool where desire boils in the deep waters," she whispered. "I dip my cup and let him drink." She paused for a minute, as the brush became caught in her hair, and untangled the knot with her fingers. Then she continued. "Without me, he cannot eat, nor drink, nor sleep, nor breathe."

She reached out to caress the picture of Alika gently with her thumb. "May desire flow through his veins and seep into his bones until he thirsts for me."

Evelyn knew the words by heart. They had become automatic, like the Bible verses she'd had to memorize at St. Bernadette's School for Girls, verses she could recite without the slightest understanding of their meaning. Today, though, she thought carefully about the words, considered their significance as she spoke, enunciated clearly.

Evelyn had found the boiling desire spell where she found all her spells and potions, on the Internet at the library. She first came across them while she was surfing the Net, seeking advice about how to manage the problem of her spectral brother. She'd been surprised to find so many sites devoted to the supernatural. There were thousands of pages offering magic spells, especially love spells, and Evelyn had been practising them diligently ever since Alika met Wendy last summer. None of them had ever worked, though. The Internet sites all promised surefire results, and many featured true-life testimonials from women who were now happily married. But in Evelyn's case, the spells seemed to have the opposite effect. The harder she tried to control the course of events, the worse things got. Last August, when she tried out the love spell with the vial of onyx oil that cost her thirty-two dollars, Alika bought Wendy a diamond ring. In October, when Evelyn pricked her finger and used her own blood in a potion, Wendy married him. All winter long, just before every full moon, Evelyn had attempted a different ritual, hoping to perfect her technique, but when spring came, there was Wendy, still living in the house that should have belonged to Evelyn, planting a garden that must have been bewitched. Evelyn would crouch in that garden some evenings, watching Alika and Wendy through the kitchen window. After they ate their dinner and cleared the table, they'd play cards or, worse, the two of them would simply sit and talk together, and Evelyn could hear them laughing. She suspected they were laughing about her.

This morning, however, Evelyn's spell would be infused with new power. After last night, her chances had surely increased. She felt a sharp spurt of exultation in her heart.

—

Noni wanted to pray, if only she could remember how. Was Alika praying? He sat in the waiting room with his head bent low, but he didn't say a word.

When Noni and Alika were children, they had rarely prayed. Their dad had been raised by Hawaiian parents, who practised an extremely relaxed form of Buddhism, and Rosa had been raised by a Catholic French-Canadian mother and an Italian socialist father who was a staunch atheist, so their religious education, though never dull, had been confusing. Noni snorted involuntarily when she recalled Detective Felix Delano and his desire to discover their ethnic identity. When you find out, she thought, let me know. As for Wendy, it was anybody's guess. Whoever

Wendy's parents were, they hadn't bothered to pass along that information.

Nor had they passed along any medical information, which was what Noni told the surgeon who wanted her history. Was there any diabetes in the family, heart disease, epilepsy? No one knew. Whatever had caused Wendy's fall remained a mystery.

Wendy was in surgery now, and Noni tried not to think about what was happening to her. All she knew was that Wendy had a serious head wound. She wanted to wait for a progress report before she called her mother, but by noon there was still no news, and she couldn't put it off any longer.

"I'm going to call Mum," she told her brother. He nodded—the first sign that he'd heard anything she'd said all day.

Rosa took the news calmly. "Don't worry," she told her daughter on the phone. "Everything is going to be all right. I'll come down right away. I'll bring some—what do you need?"

"Nothing."

"Have you eaten yet? You haven't had breakfast, have you?"

"Not yet, we—"

"Go to the cafeteria. Get yourself something nourishing. Then go straight to the hospital chapel. I'll be there as soon as I can."

Noni hung up. Her stomach growled. Rosa was right. She had to eat if she was going to get through this— whatever this turned out to be. Coffee and Aspirins would not sustain her. She needed food, something full of sugar.

—

Most people don't believe in ghosts. I found that out the hard way. When I sat down beside Noni in the hospital cafeteria, she looked right at me, but when I reached out to touch her, she shied away. She turned red, as if ashamed to be seen with me, and hurried away without finishing her pudding. It looked like very good pudding, too, chocolate, with whipped cream on top, and I realized I was hungry. I hadn't eaten a thing since yesterday. I followed Noni down the hall to the waiting room, trying to tell her what had happened to me, but she wouldn't listen. She put her hands up over her ears, to blot out my voice, and started to cry, so I left her alone.

I had figured out what had happened, though. I'd been confused at first, but now it was all starting to make sense. While I was lying there on that stretcher, staring at the ceiling of the ambulance, I remembered everything. Well, almost everything—it was impossible to concentrate. The ambulance was speeding and the sirens were blaring, a hideous noise. Then the emergency ward, alarm and dismay and shouting and terrible mess all around me. I put up with it for a while, but when they laid me out on that operating table, I knew I'd reached my limit. I never could stand the sight of blood.

So I'd come out into the corridors, looking for my family.

—

"Get anything else out of the husband?" Paul asked Felix. The detectives were standing at the top of Wendy's stairs, examining the scene, trying to concoct a theory of how she had fallen.

"Nothing," Felix said. "What do you make of him?"

Paul shrugged. "In shock, I guess." He ran his hand over the carpet, checking for a lump, a loose thread, anything that might have caused her to trip. "Think he pushed her?"

"I don't know." Felix looked into the open door of the hall closet. He saw shoes and boots, a broken kite, camping equipment. Winter clothing hung from hooks along the inner wall. "This is where she got the parka," he said. "Look."

Down below, they heard a pounding on the door.

"Maybe someone knocked on the door?" Paul suggested. "She was in the nude—sleeping, or in the shower, and she grabbed the parka."

"But it was so hot last night—even with the rain," Felix said. "Why a parka? There's plenty of summer clothing in her room. If she was trying to cover up, she was in a big hurry." He headed down the stairs to answer the door. On his way, he tested the railing. Solid.

"Larry's Locks," said the man at the door. "Sorry I'm late." He was wearing a blue uniform and carried a toolbox. "You had a break-in, right?"

"Come in," Felix said. He pulled the man gently by his sleeve. "We need to talk." He glanced outside. A couple of nosy neighbours still remained on the street, reporting the news to those who had missed the excitement. He could never get used to the way people gathered and gawked at the scenes of accidents or crimes. He was always disgusted by these hangers-on, these ungrateful fools. It was almost as if they were hoping for some kind of tragedy to make their day. A movement in the lilacs beside the house caught Felix's eye. Jesus. One of them was right in the yard. Felix decided to throw a scare into him. "Wait here a minute," he said to the locksmith.

He walked down the path. "Who's there?"

A short, slim man, about twenty-two years old, emerged from behind the bush.

"What are you doing there?" Felix demanded.

"Just, um, curious. I saw the ambulance and all and—"

"You live around here?" Felix asked him.

"Just passing through. On my way to the swimming pool, you know, to—"

Felix looked at him sternly. "Yeah, well, what's your name?"

"Marty Smith."

"You got any identification on you?"

"Sure." Marty Smith fumbled with his wallet and produced a birth certificate and social insurance card. Felix took note of them and told the man to be on his way.

"Is she all right?" Marty called, as Felix returned to the house.

Felix wheeled around. "Who?"

"The—the girl. You know. I saw them take her away in the ambulance. Is she all right?"

"We don't know yet," Felix said. He slammed the door on his way in.

When Noni returned to the waiting room, she saw a doctor in a green gown speaking to her brother. She couldn't see the doctor's face. He was sitting beside Alika, leaning forward earnestly, with his hand on Alika's arm. It was bad, then. Noni slowed her footsteps. She wasn't ready. A line from the Bible ran through her head. *I will fear no evil.* But she did fear it.

"Tell me," she said, as she approached the two men.

The doctor looked up. "Wendy sustained a fracture to her skull," he said. "An injury we might have been able to treat, if we had seen her sooner. But now—we're just doing what we can, trying to relieve the pressure, reduce the swelling."

"Can we talk to her?"

He shook his head. "She's still unconscious."

"Is it—how bad is it?" Noni asked.

"It's not good," the doctor said. "I can't promise you anything."

Alika stood up then and walked away from them.

"We're doing all we can," the doctor said quietly. He stood up, too, and Noni could see how weary he was.

"I know you are," she said.

—

I watched over my grieving husband, wanting to comfort him, but we were on two different planes. I could only follow him as he paced the tiled floors, silent and expressionless. He walked down one corridor and up another, turning corners or retracing his steps only when he met an obstacle. He was restless, the way he always was when I was late and he didn't know what to do without me. Left on his own, he was helpless. I wasn't sure how much he understood about what was going on. I tried to explain to him what had happened, to describe the way things were now, but it was an impossible task. Alika just kept striding through the halls, as if he believed he could walk

*his way back to me. He couldn't hear me. Unlike Noni, he
didn't seem to be aware of me at all. He paused at the fourth-
floor window and looked out across the river. What was he
thinking? He was as unreadable, as deliciously dense and closed
to me as ever.*

—

Whenever the mayor's wife went downtown to play the
video lottery terminals at Casey's bar, she wore a disguise.
In the ordinary course of any day, all she had to do was
take off her hat in order to disguise herself, because everyone
recognized the mayor's wife by her hats. In summer, she
wore a floppy straw affair, with a wide brim that concealed
her face. Always. With a matching bag. Without the straw
hat, nobody ever recognized her. She strolled the streets
downtown, shopped and ate in restaurants alone,
completely incognito. Nobody knew what she really looked
like. Nobody had ever bothered to take note.

But when she went to Casey's, Louise took extra care
to change her appearance. She tied her hair back tight,
placed a brown wig on her head, and covered it up with a
baseball cap. Then she dug in her gym bag for something
casual. Sweats, maybe. Something baggy. She painted her
face, heavy on the eyeliner and mascara. She placed a
cigarette behind her ear, kicked on some beat-up runners.
Then she raided the joint savings account or sometimes,
when she'd run that into the ground, the retirement bonds.

She went alone, on a bus, so that nobody would notice
her. None of the people who really knew Louise would be
caught dead on a transit bus. And there were few enough
who really knew her, anyway. Aside from the society
functions she was forced to attend, she kept to herself. She

often repeated that. "I wouldn't know," she'd say, when pressed for gossip. "I keep to myself."

One of Louise's favourite ways of keeping to herself was to fake a migraine. In fact, she was faking one this afternoon. She was, at this very moment, as she placed another load of coins into the slot, supposed to be lying down in her dark, locked bedroom with a cold cloth across her brow.

This morning, when she'd said she was jogging around Assiniboine Park, Louise had been lying in Mr. Bradley Byrnes's bed, with Mr. Bradley Byrnes. She had let him seduce her one night in the back seat of a limousine after a charity ball. That was three long years ago, and she'd been sleeping with him ever since. At first, she'd been thrilled by his attentions. She admired his impeccable taste in clothing and fine wine, revelled in his generosity. He was always willing to help out with a loan when she was short. He was a prominent citizen with his own consulting firm, so she'd been flattered when he asked for her advice on business matters or her opinion on municipal affairs. Lately, however, she was growing uneasy about Bradley Byrnes. His constant questions about City Hall bored her, and his increasing demands alarmed her. Yet she was unable to refuse him. After three years, she owed him a lot of money.

So much money that she could never hope to pay him back. At least not in cash.

Unless she got lucky. Extraordinarily lucky. And she knew that wasn't going to happen on these crummy little machines. All she was hoping for today was to win enough to replenish the household account before her husband decided he needed another summer suit. He'd been complaining lately that his green linen was getting worn.

And last month, he'd started in about a new car. A convertible he wanted! Did he think he was twenty years old again?

She punched the buttons on the VLT with determination. Today was a lucky day. August twenty-second. August was the eighth month, and the two twos made four, and Louise was forty-eight, so she just had to win.

—

Rosa's grey eyes peered sternly over her glasses at her daughter. "If something terrible was going to happen, don't you think I'd sense it?" she asked.

"I guess so," said Noni. She was a little doubtful on that score. She looked at the silver cross on the wall of the hospital chapel and wondered what it felt like to have faith. She closed her eyes and tried to commune with God, or at least to visualize Him, but she was receiving nothing. Only a dull throb where her knee had been, and a sickening ache in her near-empty stomach.

Rosa hadn't spoken to Alika yet. She'd wanted to light a candle for Wendy first. Noni watched her mother's stout body bending to the task, selecting the candle, murmuring the prayer in French.

"I want to be able to tell Alika I've done something, at least," Rosa said. "Then, if we can't see Wendy, we'll take him home. Has he eaten anything?"

"Nothing. And he hasn't slept. He worked all night at the studio."

"Then we'll go home and cook. He has to eat," Rosa said. "We all have to keep healthy. Wendy is going to need us."

"Mum," said Noni. "I think you should know. The doctor says Wendy might not make it."

"Might not make it? Make what?" Rosa began to walk toward the door, but Noni put a hand on her arm to stop her.

"Mum? I mean it. He said it doesn't look good."

Rosa stared at her daughter. "You should know better than to talk like that," she said. "Didn't I teach you anything?" But instead of leaving the chapel, she returned to the altar to select another candle.

As Noni watched her mother's broad back bending again over the thin flame, she was overcome with tenderness for her, and with a feeling of abandonment. Who would listen to Noni's fears? Behind her, the chapel door swung open, but no one entered. The door swayed back and forth and then stood still. Noni felt a sudden urge to leave the chapel. It was cold in here, and the silence was suffocating.

—

I drifted down to the chapel to look for my mother-in-law, because I thought that at least Rosa, of all people, would believe. But no—there she was, lighting a candle and concentrating so hard on her prayers she couldn't hear me. I adored Rosa. She was my favourite mother of all, the one I'd hoped to keep forever. But it annoyed me to see her lifting her eyes to the ceiling in supplication, when I was right there beside her. I felt ignored.

I wished I could leave the building, and the minute I made that wish I discovered how effortless it was. The ground dropped out from under me like a trap door, and I rose as if filled with helium. The air parted before my open arms, buoying me up as if it were water, and I swam, I sailed, I flew through the stained glass window of the chapel, over the forks of the rivers and above the trees. I knew I could keep on rising forever, through the clouds and beyond the sky. The whole earth fell away from me, relieving me of my house, my work, my entire city, even my own name, and for a long moment I floated free of it all, letting the story of my life unravel behind me. But then suddenly I wanted to gather it up again. I wanted to tell someone what had happened to me. It was a sad story, and the sadness pulled me down, back among the rooftops and the lampposts downtown. I could see the traffic in the streets. It was rush hour, everyone going home from work, except for me. I didn't have a home anymore.

To comfort myself, I visited all of my mothers—Mrs. Kowalski and Mrs. Keller and Mrs. Richards and even old Mrs. Lamb in the nursing home. Mrs. Lamb was close to the end of her life and she could see me. She smiled and nodded when I entered her room. But she was deaf now, and senile, and hadn't recognized me for years. I looked in on a few old friends I'd neglected since my marriage. I dropped by the library and listened to my substitute reading the children The Little Mermaid—the Disney version, of all things. I wandered through the city. I eavesdropped. I spied on everyone.

But it was Evelyn I was really interested in. She was the one who had murdered me.

3

THE WANDERER

I went over to Evelyn's apartment and checked to see what she was up to. She was sitting at her kitchen table, wearing a pair of green flannel pyjamas and filing her nails. When she finished, she pulled a cigarette out of her package and placed it between her lips. I was dying for a smoke. I waited for her to light a match, so that at least I could smell the burning tobacco, but she was taking her sweet time. She pulled a movie magazine out of her purse and flipped through the pages. She picked up the matches and tore one from the paper book.

Then she changed her mind. She removed the cigarette from her mouth and laid it on the table. She stood up and stretched. She opened the freezer and took out a carton of vanilla ice cream. The cardboard was lightly frosted with little crystals misting the picture on the package, two pale, creamy scoops in a blue bowl. Memory shot through me like a toothache. Ice cream. Cigarettes. I used to keep our cigarettes in the freezer, and they always tasted best when they were cold.

Evelyn dug a spoon deep into the carton and stood over the kitchen sink, licking at it delicately. Eat it, I wanted to say, scoff it up for heaven's sakes, but she ate like a kitten. She didn't appreciate anything she had. What could you expect from a murderer?

She put the ice cream back in the freezer, drank a glass of water, and sat down to light the cigarette. I watched her inhale, imagining the circulation of the smoke through the lungs, the gathering of nicotine into the bloodstream. I thought I'd go crazy if I couldn't get some nicotine into me. I thought about her crime and how she'd be punished for it. Alika would see, finally, what she was really like. Noni had been right. Evelyn was dangerous. She was one of those grasping, lethal little people who didn't know when to let go. She was greedy. I might have felt sorry for her if it weren't for everything she'd stolen from me. I had nothing, and Evelyn still had everything. I'd heard that she had no family, and I knew she'd lost Alika. But she still had flannel pyjamas and vanilla ice cream. She had a stove and a refrigerator and a huge poster on the wall of the Rocky Mountains, snow-capped peaks and a little stream running down the mountainside. An ad for beer. She probably had beer in the fridge, too. She was smoking a cigarette and reading a magazine, and I was exiled out here.

I watched her get ready for bed. She brushed her hair slowly, at least a hundred strokes. It was revolting. I consoled myself with the thought that she would be arrested soon. I had

*a detective for a neighbour, and he liked me. I could tell. He
didn't suspect her yet, but he'd soon catch on. She was so obvious.
She had a picture of Alika right beside her bed.*

—

"Mark?" said Evelyn. She whirled around in her chair. But
she knew it wasn't her brother. Not tonight. Some other
entity was prowling in the dusk outside her window.
Something she couldn't see. She jumped into bed and pulled
up the covers. What was out there? A mere wisp of a thing,
too insubstantial to be glimpsed, was watching her. Was it
malevolent? Evelyn hoped she hadn't summoned it herself,
by mistake somehow. She remembered Sister Theresa's
warnings about the occult arts, about fooling around with
the dark side. She kept her bedside lamp on all night long,
and all night long, the weak, invisible presence hovered at
the glass.

Evelyn knew what it was like to be invisible. She'd been
invisible herself, when she was a teenager. After Mark's
death, she'd come home from school every day as usual
and said hello to her mother, but her mother's eyes were
always turned toward the window or the television, or she'd
stare at the clock, astonished that her daughter was home
already, that so much time had passed. Evelyn tried to
engage her mother in conversation, but her mother always
wandered away, muttering that she'd be right back. If she
sought her out, she'd find her lying on Mark's bed, in a
deep sleep. Evelyn was old enough to take care of herself,
so she did.

It was only at bedtime that Evelyn grew insistent. At
bedtime, she begged her mother to tuck her in, even though
she was fourteen now, too old for such baby rituals. She
would turn out the light and then take hold of her mother's

hand, drawing it close to her, inhaling the scent of lavender bath salts on her skin. Evelyn held the hand tightly, kept it tethered to the bed while she talked, relating every detail of her day, because in the dark she could pretend that her mother was listening. In the dark, she couldn't see that blank face, that preoccupied glaze across her mother's eyes.

Shortly after Evelyn's fifteenth birthday, her father moved away to live with another woman, a colleague of his, who'd been transferred to Vancouver. He requested a transfer too, and the bank gave it to him. He spent two days packing and then he was gone.

During those two days, Evelyn's parents didn't speak to each other at all except to argue about Mark's things. Her father wanted a lot of photographs and some of Mark's books, but her mother wanted his room to remain exactly as it was. One day when Evelyn came home from school she heard them fighting over Mark's magic kit, her mother screaming that she had bought it for him and her father claiming that he was the one who'd taught Mark how to do the tricks. Finally, Evelyn's father called her into the bedroom and thrust the magic kit into her arms.

"Let her have it, then," he said, as if he'd forgotten his daughter's name. "That'll settle it."

Evelyn took the magic kit into her room and opened it up. Its various compartments held coins and cards, foam rubber rabbits, interlocking cups, colourful scarves, ropes, handcuffs. When Mark was alive, she'd tried to learn some of the tricks, but she'd been hopelessly inept, and he had only laughed at her. The one trick she had longed to master—the one that Mark performed with easy grace— was making the coins disappear in the magic box. Mark could place a dime in the slot and close the box. Then open it. Gone. But no matter how long or how hard Evelyn tried, the dime remained. She could not get rid of it. She could never understand the inner machinations of things, the way her brother could. He had taken the box apart once, to discover how it worked, and she remembered the way he nodded his head as he examined it, as if to say, *ah ha!* But he'd glued it back together again without disclosing its secrets. He kept the knowledge to himself, bragged of it. If he could build a box big enough, he said, he could make himself disappear.

Evelyn's parents divided up the photographs of Mark, his sports pennants, his toys. Not a word was said about the custody of Evelyn. She stayed with her mother. Not because her mother had won any arguments about it, but because nobody said anything about her. That was the way it was.

Her father called a taxi to take him to the airport, and he hugged Evelyn before he got into it.

"I'll miss you," he said. He was facing in Evelyn's direction, but he was seeing right through her. She had become transparent. She was made entirely of glass now, and she could feel a crack opening up inside her chest, beginning to split her in two.

—

The three coins lay scattered on the table top where he'd left them yesterday morning. Felix hesitated at the entrance to the porch, tempted to gather them up and toss them, to continue from the moment when Paul's call had interrupted the reading. But instead he returned to the kitchen to put on the kettle. There was no way to complete the reading now. The wind had shifted, the patterns of change had done their work.

Felix kept the loose green tea in a tin canister which Alice had given him because she knew he liked Chinese art. Felix liked Chinese everything, although he'd never been to China. He lifted the canister from the windowsill and admired it while he waited for the kettle to boil. On a black background, a scene had been etched and coloured in fine lines. An ancient Chinese gentleman in a gold and red robe sat at the foot of a blossoming tree, while a chubby little boy hurried toward him, bowing as he ran, carrying a red bowl with golden chopsticks peeking out at the top. Two elegant ladies in silver pyjamas fanned themselves gracefully with ornate folding fans, and gazed at Felix with mild interest. They inclined their heads slightly toward each other, as if they were gossiping about him. The scene was interrupted on one side by a label providing instructions for the proper preparation of the tea. Felix liked to read these words: "Be sure your teapot (an earthenware one is best) is clean and warm. Add fresh drawn water that has been brought to a furious boil." He also liked to lift the tin and read the words stamped into the bottom: "Container Made in England."

The water came to a furious boil, and Felix removed the kettle from the stove. In the silence, he could hear the clicking of the keys from Alice's room.

Alice was writing a book. Every morning from nine until noon she sat before the keyboard in her study, typing and ceasing to type in a completely unpredictable rhythm. Felix found this comforting. It was like listening to the private movements of her brain. He could tell when she was seized with an idea or when she was hovering, hesitating, trying to coax the right word to surface in her memory. Sometimes at these moments he would hold his breath, waiting for the noise to begin again.

Alice had been an unexpected gift. She was an ambitious young journalist when Felix first met her, back in the days when he'd never dreamed she'd look at a man like him, ten years older than her and already prematurely aged with weariness. But he looked at her. And about five years ago, when she covered a case he was working on, he fell irrevocably in love with her. The case was a double murder out on the Perimeter Highway—almost a triple murder, for Felix had very nearly been killed during the car chase. He likely would have died, he thought, if Alice hadn't come to the hospital every day, bringing him cards and soup, encouraging him to walk again. The sheer surprise had kept him alive.

Now, Alice had taken a leave of absence from the newspaper so that she could write a true-crime book about the case. She was writing about the year of Felix's deepest trauma and his deepest joy, and she was doing it without him. He had hinted, several times, that he was willing to read her drafts, but she always just smiled, as if she didn't even hear him. And lately it was getting worse. She spoke to her husband, when she spoke at all, in an absent-minded tone about trivial matters—the insulation, the life insurance. When he spoke to her, she seemed utterly absorbed, as if listening with intense concentration, but not to him. She seemed to be keeping a secret that he couldn't crack.

Sometimes Felix wondered if he really had died that day on the Perimeter Highway, and everything that followed—the pain, the convalescence, recovery, his life with Alice—was a kind of happy afterlife. Because sometimes he felt tenuous, as if he were not really here or as if he'd woken up inside the wrong body. There seemed to be an awful lot of room inside his body now. He felt he barely filled it up.

—

I supposed I was partly to blame for my own condition. I should have read the symptoms, figured out what she was up to. After all, I couldn't claim to be ignorant about obsession. When I was in grade seven, I'd been followed for months by the man who delivered groceries from the supermarket. He came by one Saturday with a box of charcoal briquettes, when I was home alone. It was raining that day, and he was wet, so I made him a cup of hot chocolate. He was interested in the poems I was writing—a task my English teacher had assigned. They were spread out across the kitchen table and he sat there and read them while he drank his cocoa, and asked me a lot of questions about them, which I couldn't answer. When my foster father came home, he wasn't pleased. He told me afterwards I shouldn't talk to strangers, I shouldn't let them into the house. I didn't argue, I never argued, but I didn't obey him either. I was too young to understand why I should. I let the delivery man in again several times, on Saturday afternoons when no one was home. He liked my poems and told me that I had real talent and that he should know, because he'd studied literature at the university. My poems were mostly about squirrels and lost mittens and those kinds of things. But he said I had a way of rhyming words that moved him. I'd never moved anybody before. He also helped me with math, explaining negative numbers and repeating decimals so that I actually comprehended them, and my grades began to improve.

The delivery man's name was Danny. He was a lumbering, awkward fellow of twenty-five, too old to be hanging around the kitchen with me when my parents weren't home. Gradually, I came to realize this. There was something wrong with Danny. I stopped letting him in. I hid when he knocked on the door, pretending not to be home. That was when he started to send me his own poems. He printed them out with coloured pencils on foolscap, using different colours in order to emphasize certain words, like breasts *and* blood *and* the blade of the knife. *He stashed these poems among the groceries he delivered, and one day my father found one under a sack of potatoes.*

My parents complained to the grocery manager, and Danny was fired, but this only made things worse. He started to call on the telephone, so that my parents had to change their number. He showed up at my school, followed me on my paper route, stood on my parents' front lawn in the middle of the night, demanding to see me. The police spoke to him, but it did no good. Nothing deterred him.

Finally, my parents hit on the only solution. They called my social worker, and after a serious conference, decided to transfer me to another home. I ended up in another house in another neighbourhood, attending a new school all the way across town. Danny never found me.

But how could I have avoided Evelyn? Even if I'd seen how crazy she was, I couldn't have escaped her. It wasn't possible to move out and find a new husband, the way you could find new parents. Marriage didn't work that way, or at least I didn't think it should. I'd been stuck with Alika, wanted to be stuck with him. We'd been married almost a whole year, and I'd wanted to stay married the rest of my life. I loved him, terribly. And I loved his house. I loved the garden, with its fragrant, terrible disorder. I loved the earthworms, the bumblebees, even the weeds and the mosquitoes. I loved Noni, with her round, serious face and her artificial limb, and Rosa, with her flawed psychic power. Come to think of it, here was another disaster Rosa had failed to foresee. It was Noni who'd warned me, who'd shivered.

—

By the time Evelyn was sixteen, it was clear that her mother could no longer look after herself. In one of her rare lucid periods, Evelyn's mother realized she had better return to the home of her own parents, in England. But first she arranged to have Evelyn boarded at St. Bernadette's School for Girls in St. Boniface. "Of course you don't want to leave home, dear. You wouldn't want to leave your friends," she murmured.

Evelyn didn't have any friends, but her mother didn't know that. She took Evelyn down to St. Bernadette's and introduced her to the principal, Sister Theresa, who assured them both that Evelyn would be very happy there.

St. Bernadette's was housed in an old convent that was no longer active, due to a lack of nuns. It was a beautiful old stone building, close to downtown, with spacious grounds, manicured hedges, and a soccer field. The dorms were clean and bright, and the girls they saw seemed happy, but Evelyn hated it. There was a yellow plaster Jesus hanging on a cross on the wall right above the bed that was reserved for her. His ribs stuck out, and he was bleeding bright red drops from the wound in his emaciated side.

"Don't make me go there," she begged her mother later when they were back at home. "I want to go with you."

Evelyn's mother patted her back and said, "I know, dear." Then she had to go and lie down again, in Mark's room.

Evelyn phoned her father in Vancouver and explained the situation, but he didn't offer to rescue her. "Your mother's right," he said. "It's not fair to uproot you. And her parents can hardly be expected to cope with a teenager at their age."

—

Paul and Felix tried to recreate the event at the Li residence. Had Wendy been assaulted? Had she surprised a burglar? According to the locksmith, she'd been worried about someone trespassing in her house, but she hadn't filed a police report.

Paul had theories. Maybe Alika had staged an earlier break-in to make it seem that his wife was being stalked, to throw suspicion off himself before he tried to kill her.

That didn't make sense, Felix countered. Otherwise, Alika would have mentioned the break-in to the cops. He would have played it up.

Maybe Alika hired someone to kill his wife—someone whose previous attempt had failed, Paul speculated. For her money.

Felix shook his head. He doubted Wendy Li had any money, and he was pretty sure this wasn't a case of premeditation. If Alika was guilty, it was a spur-of-the-moment thing, the usual domestic violence.

When they finally caught up with Alika at the hospital and drove him downtown for an interview, the results were inconclusive. Paul took the aggressive role, firing personal questions about the marriage, the finances, whether there was a history of violence, whether Wendy was seeing another man. He was trying to rattle Alika, get a rise out of him, but as far as Felix could tell, Alika showed no guilt. He didn't even seem to grasp the intent of the questions. Once or twice, a quizzical expression passed across his features. The question about Wendy's possible lover provoked a wrinkle of the forehead and a sudden excess of politeness, as if Paul were inquiring whether she'd ever been abducted by aliens. But otherwise, Alika was passive—still stunned, Felix guessed, by the consequences of Wendy's fall.

But had she fallen? Could such a thing happen? An ugly panorama of accident scenes flashed through his memory—chainsaws, automobiles, rifles, electrical wires, deep, deep water. Surely Wendy would recover. Felix couldn't imagine anyone so young and healthy simply stumbling to her death in her own home.

—

I'd never really been religious, even though I'd been baptized twice. Once by Mrs. Keller, who was Catholic, and once by Mrs. Richards, who got born again one summer and had all nine of her foster children baptized at a revival meeting one Sunday just before they took us all away from her. I didn't think Alika's family was religious either. But it seemed that whenever I looked in on Rosa, she was praying for me. I guess she was trying to cover all the bases, and I appreciated it, though I wasn't sure exactly what she was asking for. Watching her, I wondered what she hoped to accomplish. Did she want me to come back? Or did she want me to move on?

I knew I could move on, leave the earth. I had nearly done it that first day when I rose into the sky. But every time I flew too high, saw the earth so far away from me, I heard those other voices calling, and I grew uneasy. I came back to my home, my husband. I had responsibilities. I couldn't leave Alika. And there was no way I was going to let Evelyn get away with this. So I stayed close to the old neighbourhood. I patrolled St. Catherine Street, roaming from house to house, checking up on my family and on Felix. With so much time on my hands, I realized there were a lot of beautiful things in my neighbourhood, things I'd passed by every day when I was alive and never appreciated, like the tree on the corner.

At the very end of St. Catherine Street, in front of Felix's house, a huge silver maple spread out over the sidewalk, so that pedestrians had to push aside its lower branches to pass by. The first day I visited Felix at home, he was contemplating that tree from an upstairs window of his house. I could barely see him through the forest of poplars in his yard, so I rose higher, into the limbs of the silver maple. I saw a squirrel's nest there, and a pair of squirrels running up and down the trunk with seeds and acorns in their mouths. I remembered reading that squirrels worked so hard because half the time they forgot where they hid their acorns. I'd found that funny once.

Felix looked very serious, almost morose, and I imagined that he was thinking of me, of my demise. I watched him rub a palm across his forehead, pondering the problem deeply. He seemed intelligent. Dedicated to his job. Upholder of law and order. I was confident that he would set things right. But I wished I'd mentioned Evelyn to him before she got me. I wished I could report her crime like a normal person would, sitting in a police station filling out forms, pointing her out in a line-up. I'd have to leave that to others.

The wind was growing stronger. Black clouds were filling the sky. Felix Delano turned away from the window and disappeared somewhere inside his house.

I rose above the silver maple and looked down upon its crown. Its leaves were dark as iron in the evening light, and when the wind passed through its branches, it swayed and tossed, revealing the underside of its leaves, shimmering like pale sage. I had never seen it for what it truly was—a giant being, rooted to the planet, rustling and breathing. It bent its great body with the wind, bowing sometimes toward the grass and reaching sometimes toward the sky, but always it remained, anchored deep below the surface of the earth.

I envied it.

—

When she sat in the hospital room, watching Wendy's chest rise and fall with the mechanical rhythm of the respirator, Noni couldn't feel Wendy's spirit at all. She could only sense it if she was all alone—like that first day in the cafeteria, when she felt Wendy so close beside her she imagined her breath on her neck. Or when she heard the low moaning at the window—summer wind, she told herself, she should buy weatherstripping. But she knew the summer wind didn't sound like that, not unless there was a storm. And there had been no storms since the night that Wendy fell. At these times, Noni feared her sister-in-law had left her body. Had passed on.

Sometimes, early in the morning, Noni dreamed that Wendy was standing at the foot of her bed. Often the dream was so vivid it terrified her, and she woke trembling. One night she rented the movie *Hamlet* and afterwards dreamed that Wendy was spurring her on to avenge her death. Even after waking, Noni found it hard to shake the eerie sensation that Wendy was present in her apartment. She could hear

Wendy's voice in her head, whispering urgently, but she couldn't make out the words.

Was there anything to avenge?

Detective Delano seemed to think so. He came to the hospital and questioned Noni about her brother and his marriage to Wendy. Noni answered truthfully. Her brother was a gentle man, he loved his wife, they all loved her.

He assured Noni that the questions were routine. It was just that it seemed unlikely, he said carefully, that Wendy's fall had been an accident. He had examined the scene and doubted she could have tripped in the first place, he said, let alone fallen with such force, even if she'd been unconscious. He suspected Wendy had been pushed from behind, probably by a burglar.

Noni said she didn't think anything had been stolen from the house. Alika hadn't mentioned that anything was missing.

"Then is there anyone you can think of who might have wanted to hurt her?" he asked. "Anyone at all?"

Noni started to shake her head. Then she remembered.

—

Almost as soon as Evelyn James opened her door for him, Felix decided that she was probably innocent. She was tiny, for one thing, not strong enough to have committed such an assault. And it seemed she knew nothing of Wendy's fall or her coma. When Felix told her about it, she placed both hands over her mouth and stared at him with wide eyes, while the blood drained from her face. Felix thought she was going to faint.

But he still had to question her. Noni had told him about the stocking, along with some crazy theory about

Evelyn breaking in and leaving it there. If Alika had his wife and his sister believing that, he was a pretty slick liar.

"Sit down, sit down," he said. He ushered Evelyn into her own kitchen. A pot of tea sat on the table and a full cup steamed beside it. Felix guided her into a chair. "Drink your tea," he said. "It'll do you good."

She drank the tea, holding the cup with two shaking hands.

"When did this happen?" she managed to ask.

"Last Thursday. August twenty-first."

Evelyn lost her grip on the cup and it crashed down into the saucer.

Felix pulled out a chair for himself.

"Would you like some tea?" she asked. "The cups are behind you, there, on those hooks."

He reached up and took one. "Thanks. Do you have milk?" He moved toward the refrigerator, but Evelyn jumped up and stood in front of it, blocking his way.

"I'll get it," she said. She poured the milk from the carton into a tiny pitcher and set it on the table.

"Did you see Wendy on the twenty-first?" Felix asked.

"I haven't seen her for months."

"You haven't visited her house?"

"No!"

"Where were you that night?"

Evelyn glanced at the calendar on the wall. Thursday the twenty-first was marked with a circle to represent the full moon. "I worked the late shift until eleven and then I came home to bed."

"Alone?"

"Yes."

"What were you doing? Watching television?"

"I don't remember."

"Did you talk to anyone that night, on the phone, maybe?"

"I don't remember." Her voice had dropped to a whisper.

Felix looked hard at the girl's pale face. She was definitely shocked by this news. Even if she was having an affair with the husband, she honestly didn't seem to have a clue about Wendy's fall.

"How is Alika taking it?" she asked.

"Not very well," said Felix.

—

Alika stood at the living room window, watching the empty street. He often stood staring at nothing, and sometimes I used to stand behind him, trying to see what he was looking at. I could never tell, especially when he was taking pictures. He'd hold the camera to his eye, look at the world through that one hole. What did he see?

This morning, he had dressed carelessly. His collar buttons were crooked, and I wanted to reach out and put them right. I wondered if he'd misbuttoned his shirt all the way down, and I moved closer to the window, trying to see his whole body. I pushed up close against the glass and then I found myself inside the house. I was right there in the living room with him. I was back!

"Alika," I said. "I'm home." But he didn't believe me. He placed his right palm against the pane and leaned forward,

gazing across the lawn, as if he were looking for me, waiting for me to return.

I pressed myself against his chest, the way I'd pressed against the window glass, but I could not enter him. I had never been able to enter him fully.

—

The pile of clothing next to Noni's sewing machine remained untouched. She couldn't face it yet. Like Alika, she was finding it hard to focus on the details of her regular routine. Gino had granted Alika a leave of absence from the studio, but Noni had no one to give her time off. Her work just sat there—bundles of torn dress shirts, jeans that wanted hemming, skirts that needed letting in or letting out. This morning, Noni barely glanced at them. She'd spent the night at Alika's house and this morning she'd come home only to shower and change while her mother shopped for groceries. Then they were going back to Alika's for brunch. Rosa was determined to keep on cooking. As if cooking would help. That's what people did during disasters.

Alika seemed relieved to see them. Noni couldn't tell what he'd been doing before they arrived, but he certainly hadn't made any preparations for brunch. Rosa set to work cracking and beating the eggs, while Noni washed dishes and set the table. The kitchen was small and they bumped into each other as they worked. Still, the room seemed empty without Wendy. The whole scene felt artificial. Rosa chatted with forced cheer, suggesting that Alika pick some flowers from the garden. They would take a bouquet to Wendy this morning, she said. It had been a week, now. Surely Wendy would wake up today. Alika looked out at the garden. He made no move to go outside.

Rosa whipped up a mushroom omelette and served it with toast and jam. Nobody ate much, not even Rosa, though she made a pretense, pushing the food about on her plate. After an interminable silence, she rose and began to gather the plates. She briskly washed and rinsed them, scoured the pan, wiped the counter. Noni remained at the table, beside Alika. She tried to catch his eye, but he wouldn't turn away from the window. She reached out and pressed his hand. He responded with a slight, distracted pressure.

"You need to take out the garbage," Rosa told her son.

He didn't move.

"Alika," warned Rosa. "I'm talking to you."

"It can wait, Mum," said Noni gently. "The trucks don't come until tomorrow."

Rosa lifted the bag from the trash pail, twisted it shut, and held it toward her son. "They might come early," she said.

Noni sighed. She took the bag and carried it through the garden. She dumped it in the can and placed the lid on firmly, to keep the dogs away during the night.

The storm clouds that had gathered the night before had blown over before it rained, and the garden was dry. Noni stopped to run her hand through the long stems of the poppies. They were long past blooming now, and their seed pods rattled in the morning breeze. She ripped one from its stem and held it in her hand. She could feel how frail it was, and it made her angry. She crushed it to powder.

The wind was gathering strength. It moaned through the neighbour's elm trees, causing the leaves to murmur with the cadence of a human voice. Noni shuddered.

As she hurried back toward the house, she heard the grinding gears of a city garbage truck as it turned into the lane.

—

I could see Noni out in the back lane. She was bending over the tall stalks of the poppies, examining their round seed husks. She plucked one and crumbled it between her fingers, letting the half-formed seeds fall to the ground.

"Noni," I said, and she looked up.

"They're not ready yet," I told her. "Wait for the fall."

She turned away from me then and started toward the house, the wind whipping her short, dark hair across her face.

"Wait!" I called, but this only seemed to make her move faster. She limped quickly, awkwardly, up the back steps and then paused for a minute, listening nervously, before she went into the house.

I didn't want to scare Noni, but I missed her. She was the only one who would understand about Evelyn. And she was a good friend, a sister. My only sister. I'd had a few foster sisters and brothers along the way, but they were always coming and going. I'd learned pretty early that it wasn't wise to get too close to them. One or another of them was always getting returned to their real parents. I knew that was never going to happen to me. My real parents had given me away. The trouble was, they hadn't given me to anyone. I was sort of adrift.

So I had given myself to Alika and his family. I'd thought it was safe. But after one short year, Evelyn had taken me away from them.

—

The beauty of the *Book of Changes* was that Felix could never understand it. The verses were all about crossing the great water and foxes getting their tails wet, and who could make any sense of that? Every once in a while, he'd have a glimmer of comprehension, like the day he tossed a hexagram that warned him to pay attention to small, seemingly insignificant details. As a detective, he understood that. But mostly, Felix considered the tossing of the coins a kind of telling of the weather. It wasn't a guide. It was more like a barometer.

A very stoned girl in a cotton dress had given Felix the *Book of Changes* at the first Winnipeg Folk Festival—the free one, back in the seventies. Felix was taking an Eastern philosophy course then, and he was interested in the book's introduction. But he hadn't been tempted to toss the coins to read the hexagrams. His mother used to perform a similar rite in times of crisis or indecision, using the New Testament and a bobby pin. When Felix was in college, he'd considered that to be primitive nonsense. He believed in logic and relied on his reason to guide him. When he decided to join the police force, he welcomed the chance to put those beliefs into practice. But once he got out on the streets, once he'd been spat on and sworn at and punched and finally shot in the chest, he asked his mother to pray for him once in a while. It couldn't hurt. And now and then he tossed the coins, just to give himself something to meditate on for the day. The process had come to interest him more and more. For one thing, he'd never, in all the years he'd been reading the book, thrown the same hexagram twice. This was mathematically impossible, he knew. Yet it was true. Because every time Felix threw the coins, the wind was blowing from a different direction, the sun was shining from a different angle, and Felix was a different man.

He threw the coins six times and recorded the lines. They led him to "Innocence," which sounded good. But when he turned to the verse, the first words he saw were "Undeserved Misfortune. Misfortune from within and without." Shit. There was no mistaking the meaning of that.

He stood up, leaving the book on the table, and listened. Where was his wife? She'd promised to join him for dinner tonight, but he didn't believe her. She'd worked straight through dinner every night this week. He walked down the hallway, listening harder. Yes. Typing again.

—

Evelyn's heart had hammered in her chest when that detective gave her the news, and it was still beating faster than normal. A coma! Dear God, what had she done? Would she be arrested? She sat at her kitchen table, chain-smoking, and tried to decide what to do.

Her first instinct had been to get out of town immediately, to get away from the detective's questions and his prying eyes. But she feared that would only draw more suspicion on herself. And she had no confidence in her ability to escape. She'd tried to run away before, and she had failed.

When she was sixteen, two days before she was supposed to start classes at St. Bernadette's, Evelyn had made the first impulsive move of her short life. She stole ninety dollars from her mother's purse, packed a few things in a cardboard suitcase, went downtown and boarded a bus to Vancouver. Right up until the moment the bus pulled away from the terminal, she wasn't sure if she was really going to do it. She was nervous, worried that someone might think she was too young to be going all the way to Vancouver by herself. But nobody questioned her. Her invisibility had settled over her completely now, and no one noticed her at all. Even the driver forgot to take her ticket as she boarded the bus, and she had to thrust it at him twice before he saw it. The bus headed west down Portage Avenue, all the way to the Perimeter Highway, the farthest west she'd ever been, and just kept right on going.

Evelyn got off the bus at Brandon and then got on again, because everybody else did. All the way across the country, everybody got off every two hours to smoke or buy potato chips and stale sandwiches wrapped in plastic— even in the middle of the night. She learned to stay close to the coach and keep her eye on the driver while he drank his coffee, so she wouldn't get left behind. Sometimes she dreamed about exploring the little towns they passed through. But all she ever saw of Regina and Moose Jaw and Swift Current and Medicine Hat were the bus depots.

The bus arrived in Golden, BC, just as the sun was climbing over the horizon. Evelyn had never seen a place so cool and clean before. She'd never seen snow so white, water so clear. When she stepped off the bus she felt as if she were ascending into the blue air and the white clouds, because the sky was everywhere around her; she was inside it.

While the driver unloaded luggage and freight, Evelyn walked to the edge of the parking lot and looked into the dense brush and trees of the wooded mountainside. High above, she could see a stream rushing at white speed down the mountain, spuming into a clean blue pool below. She was mesmerized by the morning light, its pale, porous quality, the way it seemed to slide up the mountain from below, until the snow was bright as fire. She stayed so long, just looking and breathing, that she nearly missed the bus.

In Vancouver, she called her father from the depot and he came to get her in his car. He seemed angry and uncertain and wouldn't look directly at her. At home, his new wife made up a bed for Evelyn in a spare room—they had a lot of spare rooms—while her father phoned her mother to say that Evelyn was all right. Long into the night she heard her father and his new wife discussing things in serious tones and sometimes they hissed at each other.

In the morning, after her father explained that she had to go home, Evelyn went for a long walk along the seawall. She considered jumping into the Pacific, but she didn't. She went back home and repacked her suitcase, and the next day she let her father give her a lot of money and drive her to the depot and put her on the bus. It was the same bus, with the same graffiti on the backs of the seats.

It was noon when she arrived in Golden again, and the light was more intense, more spectacular than it had been the day before. The driver opened the luggage compartment and took out two bags for the two people who had reached their destination. Then Evelyn performed the second impulsive act of her life. She asked for her own luggage. She pointed to her suitcase, and the driver leaned in and hauled it out.

"It's tagged for Winnipeg," he said, but he gave it to her.

Evelyn walked across the parking lot, carrying the cardboard suitcase. It was light enough. There wasn't much in it besides a few clothes and the magic kit. And she was feeling strong, strong and light and happy to be living in the sky. She spent an hour traipsing the thin trails though the brush on the mountainside, inhaling the pure, blue air, exhilarated.

Nobody knew where she was. True, she had been alone for years, and no one had ever cared where she was, but at least this time she had chosen to be lost. Suspended high between the prairies and the ocean, between her mother and her father, she was severed at last, cut loose, unattached as her brother Mark. She was liberated.

She would stay here, she thought. Get a job, maybe at the bus depot coffee shop, or one of the stores in town, and live in the mountains, breathe this air for the rest of her life.

All afternoon she trudged through the streets of the town, asking for work. But she had no experience. She hadn't even finished high school. Nobody would hire her.

"What skills do you have?" the man at the lumberyard asked, and she couldn't even think of an answer. The afternoon wore on, the suitcase grew heavier, and she began to worry about the night. She must have been mad to get off the bus. As the sun sank lower in the sky, the mountain air grew cold. She headed back toward the depot.

The lady at the wicket told her there was an eastbound bus passing through in an hour. Evelyn sat down on the bench outside and waited. The sun was setting over the mountains. Orange flames licked the snow at the top of the peaks. She tried to tell herself she'd accomplished something unique, something valuable. She'd had nearly one whole day in Golden. She could hear the ticket agents talking in the booth behind her. One of them clucked her tongue in disgust and said, "Runaways!" in a bored, dismissive voice. And then Evelyn understood that she was not even original. She was a speck in a vast and nebulous galaxy of losers.

4

THE ABYSMAL

Fate, I thought to myself. Was this my fate? To be floating around out here all alone while Evelyn perfected her designs on my husband? For I had no doubt that was her plan. Mrs. Kowalski would have said there's no such thing as fate, that you have to make your own destiny. Was she right about that? Should I have foreseen this crime? In retrospect, the signs were plain: the perennials, the monogrammed notebook, the stocking.

I wondered how long ago this chain of events had begun and whether it had been destined to unfold this way. Alika believed that our marriage was meant to be. But he'd also once believed he was meant to be with Evelyn. That was before he'd ever laid eyes on me, he said, so it didn't count. He had first met her at the corner convenience store—nothing especially preordained about that. But then he began to run into her everywhere. He bumped into her outside his gym. He saw her at the hardware store. She even came into the studio where he worked to have some photos retouched. There must have been a reason for all that coincidence, he thought. She seemed to turn up everywhere he went, as if by magic, as if by fate. And so Alika, son of Rosa, simply surrendered.

—

Evelyn peeked out the curtains, scanning the street below for signs of a police car. She couldn't see one. Nevertheless, she was convinced she was under surveillance. And she could feel someone watching her, even when she was alone in her apartment, which was pretty much all the time, lately. It was that wistful, anaemic presence she'd first sensed outside her window a couple of weeks ago. It seemed to have invaded her apartment now, and she encountered its cold hostility and melancholic longing frequently, as she turned a corner or stepped from one room into another. It might be an evil spirit, or a wounded one. It might be somebody Evelyn once knew, somebody with something to tell her. She considered trying to exorcise it. There were plenty of chants for this purpose on the Internet. But she was wary of addressing this thing, whatever it was. She just might bond it to her by mistake. It wouldn't be the first time.

Evelyn's troubles with ghosts could be traced back about six years, to St. Bernadette's School. When she'd returned from her aborted escape to BC, nearly a week late for the beginning of term, Sister Theresa had marched her straight to her room and helped her unpack, sifting carefully through her things with disapproval. As soon as she saw the magic kit, she marched Evelyn straight downstairs again, all the way to the cellar, where she made Evelyn hold the kit open while she threw its contents, item by item, into the incinerator. When the box was empty, she burned it, too, saying there was no place here for such things, and then she sent Evelyn to confession, forgetting that Evelyn wasn't even Catholic.

The three other girls in Evelyn's dorm at St. Bernadette's were Catholics. They all professed to believe in angels and purgatory and the Resurrection. They went to confession and repeated Hail Marys for infractions such as putting chalk dust on Sister Theresa's chair. They repeated the things the priest said about hell and the punishment that awaited the wicked. But at the same time, Evelyn could tell they didn't really believe these things. If they had, they would never have behaved the way they did.

All the nuns said that fortune telling was the work of the Devil. Yet despite these warnings, the girls were fascinated by tarot cards and tea leaves and magic eight balls. During an unsupervised outing downtown, two of the more daring girls bought a Ouija board at a department store and smuggled it up to their room. Soon, even the most devout of Evelyn's dorm mates joined the group around the candle after lights-out to consult the Ouija about exam results and future husbands.

All the girls thought it was very romantic that Evelyn had a dead brother, especially a dead twin, and one night they convinced her to try contacting him through the Ouija board.

The boldest girl, whose name was Jo, placed her fingers lightly on one edge of the little planchette and persuaded Evelyn to place her own fingers on the other. Then Jo posed a question.

"Mark James, can you hear us?"

At first, nothing happened.

Jo tried again. "Mark James, can you hear us?"

Still nothing happened. Jo kept repeating the question, in a dreadful monotone, until Evelyn begged her to stop. But then the planchette gave a little jerk and began to glide toward the word *yes*. Evelyn emitted a yelp and the candle blew out. In the darkness, the other girls grabbed onto one another, terrified and thrilled. Jo struck a match and relit the wick. They stared at each other in the dim light of the candle flame.

"Try again!" Betty cried.

"No," said Evelyn.

But there was no stopping them now. They insisted. Evelyn reluctantly placed her trembling fingers back on the planchette.

"Can you hear us, Mark James?" Jo asked. "Do you have a message for your sister?"

The pointer began to move again, spelling out letters, now. Each time it spelled a word, Jo would pronounce it aloud. "*E, V*," she said. "He's spelling your name! Evelyn, look!"

Evelyn was looking. She was watching Jo very closely, to see if she was cheating. She could feel the planchette being tugged along beneath her fingers, but of course it was impossible to tell, or to prove, who might be moving it. It spelled out Evelyn's name, then paused, then headed for the *W*.

"Where!" cried Jo. "Is! My! Where is my." The pointer stopped.

"Where is my what?" asked Betty.

Evelyn had turned pale, but nobody noticed. They were caught up in deciphering the message. The pointer moved to *M*.

"Where is my mother?" Betty suggested. But the pointer moved next to *A*.

Only Evelyn knew what was coming. She watched with dread as the pointer moved from letter to letter, and then finally sat still.

"Where is my magic kit?" Jo was puzzled. "What's he talking about?"

Evelyn made no answer. She was staring at the candle, remembering the green flames that shot out of the incinerator when Sister Theresa fed it the last coloured scarf in the magic kit. It had seemed to her then a kind of cremation, a farewell. But now Mark had emerged from his long silence on the other side. How was she ever going to get him to go back?

—

Felix opened the paper and thumbed through the pages, reading about the planned expansion of the floodway, the larviciding of the ditches. He checked out his horoscope...not that Felix believed in astrology. He'd once had a few drinks with a copyreader at the *Star*, a terrible skeptic who admitted to switching the horoscopes around before they went to press, so that Cancers were reading the advice for Virgos, and Virgos were reading Scorpio. "Nothing happened," he told Felix. "Things went on as usual."

The letters on the editorial page were full of complaints about the new casino, but Felix knew this was only a ploy on the part of the newspaper. Tomorrow, the letters would be full of praise for All-Am Development and the economic boom that was sure to follow the casino opening. Felix was so bored by the new casino he couldn't read another sentence. He looked out the window for Alice's car, although he knew she wouldn't be home for another hour or so.

Alice had gone out to meet with her editor, who was getting nervous about the book deadline. The date for delivery of the manuscript had passed two months ago, and Alice was still writing. Yesterday, Felix came right out and asked her if she wanted his help, but Alice had smiled as usual and changed the subject. Now Felix got up and entered Alice's study. The manuscript was stacked neatly beside the keyboard, weighed down with the stone Buddha he'd given her on their anniversary.

It wouldn't hurt, would it? Just to take a peek?

—

If Louise didn't win today, she was in trouble. She sat at the bar, nursing her glass of ginger ale, watching the backs of all the people at the VLTs. Every single machine was taken, and Louise was keeping her eye on a skinny old man in a yellow sweater who was also waiting for a turn. Louise was five feet closer to the machines than he was, and if she kept a sharp lookout, she'd beat him to it as soon as somebody quit. She was hoping for the machine second from the left, being played by a woman in a halter top and short shorts—probably a prostitute. Louise hoped she'd get a trick and quit soon. That machine hadn't paid out for at least an hour, and if Louise was lucky, she'd be the one to collect when it did. It was all a matter of timing.

She tried not to think about Bradley Byrnes and what he wanted her to do. She'd been running all over town for him this past winter, doing little favours to pay off her debts to him, and now she wanted out. If she could just get on top of this money thing—earn enough off the VLTs to place a solid bet on the horses—maybe even get to

Vegas—she could come out so far ahead she'd never have to worry again. She could pay off Byrnes and never have to speak to him again. Her relationship with him was spiralling out of control, making her sick with anxiety.

It started off innocently enough, a couple of years ago. When she'd needed help to pay back some unfortunate loans, she'd offered Byrnes a little inside information, before the casino project was public knowledge. She told him about the proposal, making it sound like a done deal, and Byrnes had been pleased. He'd paid off her loans and then got to work buying up properties in the condemned zone. He purchased eight abandoned, dilapidated buildings from grateful owners who were glad to get rid of them at last.

But it hadn't ended there. Byrnes could have sold the buildings to All-Am for cash and walked away with a handsome profit. How Louise wished he had! Instead, he'd sold them for shares in the casino. He was a partner in it now—a silent partner, to keep attention off the speedy flip of his properties—and he was committed to the project, determined to see it succeed.

For this, he seemed to need Louise at every turn. First, there had been the trouble about the bidding—with All-Am nearly losing the contract to another company. Then City Council had hesitated on the tax breaks. Then that Historical Preservation business. Now this hassle over the injunction. And Byrnes expected Louise to take care of it all.

Finally! A woman at the far right cashed out and Louise made a bee-line for her machine. It wasn't the machine she'd wanted, but by now Louise didn't care. As long as she could get on any machine and set the process in motion. It was the only thing that kept her sane. It was better than yoga or Valium. When she was sitting in front of the VLTs, lulled by the wide bank of blinking lights, the colourful spinning fruits, the hypnotic sound of coins dropping and buttons clicking, she entered a state of serenity that lowered her blood pressure, emptied her mind. It was the only sure way she knew to keep her thoughts from circling endlessly around her marriage and her money problems—and the ungrateful children she'd raised. The two tall boys who didn't need her any more, who'd turned their backs on her and boarded airplanes to American colleges where they'd quickly turned into men like their father. Her lost babies. She couldn't bear to think about them. She gave the button a vicious jab. Come on, come on. It was her turn, goddamn it.

—

Evelyn's stomach knotted and turned over, making her groan. She was ill, too upset about that detective to be able to do her shift tonight. She couldn't stop worrying that he'd come back; she had no alibi for the night of Wendy's fall, and she knew her fingerprints must be all over Wendy's house. She called in sick to the convenience store, speaking in a raspy voice and faking a few coughs. She hoped her boss would believe she had the flu. She couldn't afford to lose her job, no matter what happened.

She'd been lucky to find this job right after she graduated from St. Bernadette's. As a graduation present, her father had offered to help with university tuition. But Evelyn had had enough of school. She didn't think she could concentrate on studies, anyway, with Mark keeping her up at night the way he did. She wished she had never called him back. He would stand outside her window, waving his wand or performing, in elaborate pantomime, the tying of knots, the palming of coins. It seemed he never tired of upbraiding her for losing the magic kit. No, she couldn't possibly muster the solitary discipline that studying required. She needed distraction. And the convenience store provided plenty of that.

The convenience store, in fact, was nothing but an endless series of distractions, urgent, trivial tasks that interrupted each other in an unbroken chain from morning to night, so that nobody who worked there could ever string together two coherent thoughts. Evelyn liked it that way. She also liked the anonymity of the place. There was a pleasant illusion of intimacy in the store, never authentic enough to be mistaken for true intimacy, and far more comforting than the real thing. Customers told her the most surprising details of their private lives, then took their newspapers or milk or coffee and simply left. Nobody asked her much about herself. She lost touch with Jo and Betty and the other girls from St. Bernadette's, most of whom went on to university. She rented a small apartment near the store and settled into a small, circumscribed life in which there was little hope and therefore little disappointment.

Among the regulars, Evelyn had a few favourites. There was the elderly widow who shoplifted tins of cat food, while Evelyn made sure to look the other way, and the firefighters from the fire hall down the street who called her "Sweetheart" and complained about their wives. Her favourite customer of all was a young man with golden skin and a glass eye, who was forever leaving behind his sunglasses or his cigarettes or his keys. Evelyn would place these objects into the lost and found box, a little off to the side, apart from the ordinary jumble of lost things, because they were special. And because she knew he would be coming back. She recognized it as a form of flirting, this constant pretense at forgetting. A way of seeing her again and again. A way of making her think of him when he was not there.

Evelyn felt a warm rush of regret, almost pleasurable, as she remembered the afternoon Alika left his wallet on the counter and changed her life forever. A wallet was a necessary item, and Evelyn expected him back any minute, but he didn't come. She opened it up and found his identification, his address—he lived in a house close by—and his telephone number. So she called him. But first, she turned the wallet inside out, perused his business cards, driver's license, gym membership, his receipts from the drycleaner and the hardware store.

"Thanks," he said, as soon as he arrived. "I didn't even notice it was missing."

Evelyn handed the wallet back to him, and he put it in his pocket without looking inside. That meant he trusted her.

"You're very kind," he said.

Evelyn tried not to show her surprise. She tried to act as if people said such things to her all the time.

"Thank you," she said. "You're very—you're beautiful." She blushed. What had possessed her to say such a thing?

Alika was looking at her intently. He was seeing her.

"When do you get off?" he asked.

"Not until eleven."

He smiled. "Should I come back at eleven?"

"Yes," she said.

For the rest of her shift, she flew through her chores, dusting and ringing up purchases and counting out change with a grin. He had noticed her. He had really seen her.

—

Alika didn't know how to cook. He was aware that cabbages and lettuce and basil and tomatoes grew in the backyard. He had, occasionally, purchased lemons, salt, and other necessities from the supermarket. But how these ingredients came together to create his meals, his home, his daily, unnoticed comforts, was a mystery to him. I watched him sadly as he ripped a piece of bread from a stale loaf, then looked at it as if he didn't know what it was for.

Now that I was gone, the house was reverting to the chaos of its bachelor state. The drain in the kitchen sink was full of tiny objects—grains of rice, twist ties, noodles, the little leaves from the Brussels sprouts. Everything that resided under the furniture—socks and books and bits of string and unpaid bills—was accumulating a thin veneer of greasy dust. And there was nothing I could do about it.

I lingered by Alika's side, longing to touch his beautiful black hair, his dark eyebrows, to trace the contours of his damaged ear. He closed his eyes, began to snore. I watched his temples, his smooth, high forehead. What on earth went on in there? I pictured the interior of my husband's mind as a dimly lit space, crowded with tangled bits of string, dusty old noodles and leftover Brussels sprouts, their tiny leaves unravelling, seeking the light.

———

Seated at Alice's desk, Felix moved his finger slowly down the pages as he read.

This wasn't him. This fearless, swift-thinking hero. He read about a decisive, risk-taking Felix, a Felix who squared his jaw and looked danger in the face, barely wincing when the bullet came searing through his chest.

Felix knew he'd screamed when the bullet hit him. Just like a girl. And he'd cried in the emergency ward, while a beautiful young doctor worked feverishly to staunch the wound, and a nurse held onto his hand. He'd wept, remembering he hadn't taken Poppy for a walk that morning, that he'd neglected to feed her, that his morning had been erased, and there was no way he was ever going to recover it.

As he read further, Felix noticed that Alice couldn't seem to keep the story on track. She kept going off on tangents, or adding details that had nothing to do with the murder case. In the third chapter, in the middle of a scene about Felix's physiotherapy, she began to describe the time he'd swum out into the middle of Falcon Lake to help a drowning boy—an event that occurred when Felix wasn't even on duty. It had happened long before the double murder, long before he'd even met Alice. It had merited only two inches of newsprint at the time, but Alice, an assiduous researcher, had found them. She had gleaned the bare facts of the incident and embroidered them wildly.

Felix remembered the occasion very well. He was on vacation and it was his birthday. Early in the evening, as the sun was sinking in an overcast sky, he'd been waiting for his friends to arrive to take him into town for a birthday dinner. He'd been hungry and a little impatient, barely paying attention to the crowd of boisterous, splashing teenagers cannonballing from the off-shore diving dock. But he happened to be watching, idly, as one of them attempted a one-and-a-half off the three-metre board. Felix saw the boy go up and up and then tuck his head into his chest, and he knew something was off. A miscalculation had been made. Felix started running even before he saw the diver's head graze the edge of the board as he came down. He was in the water before the other kids yelled for help. When Felix saw the boy in danger, Alice wrote, his first thought had been to save a life. But that wasn't true. Felix's first thought had been that the water was cold, that he didn't want to get wet, that he'd just dressed for dinner. He dived off the boat dock and swam about a hundred yards and then began to surface-dive, while the boy's parents paddled frantically in their canoe toward the spot where their son had vanished. Alice spent two long paragraphs describing that hundred-yard swim, putting all sorts of thoughts into Felix's head, about not giving up, about the value of the boy's life. The only thought Felix remembered having spared for the kid was "you idiot!" He had dived and dived again until he caught the boy by the hair and dragged him to the surface. It was an ugly business. The kid had vomited, and so had Felix. The mother had been hysterical. Felix's birthday plans were ruined. But Alice made it sound like a miracle.

Felix read again the description of his own heroism. He wanted to be fearless and swift-thinking. But he knew he wasn't. No. Alice had dreamed this story. She had made it all up, out of some deep, Irish corner of her imagination. He ran his finger lightly across the description of this other Felix, this distorted reflection. Who was this man his wife had created? Whoever he was, it was clear that Alice was falling in love with him.

—

Evelyn curled up on the couch with a hot water bottle and a quilt, just as if she really were sick, and thought about Alika. Her first date with him had been her first date ever. He picked her up at the store at eleven o'clock, just as he'd promised, and took her to an all-night doughnut shop nearby. Evelyn was too excited to eat her walnut cruller, even though Alika had bought it for her. She just sipped her soda and asked him questions about his family and his childhood in Hawaii.

"Why did you move to Canada?" she asked.

"My mother grew up here, in Winnipeg. She met my dad in Hawaii when she took a vacation there. So then, when she left him..." He shrugged.

So, he was a child of a broken home, too. They had something in common. A bond.

"Have you ever been to Golden?" she asked. She tried to tell him how the light hit the mountains there, but she couldn't get the words right. She sounded dumb, and Alika was growing distracted, bored with her.

Evelyn felt that old, panicky flutter in her chest, that feeling that she might crack in two. She had to get his attention, make him see her again. So she told him the story of her brother, Mark, and he listened. He was sympathetic, placing one of his large, warm hands over hers, sending a tingle through the veins of her arm into her heart. But afterwards he never called her. He didn't come back to the store for a whole week.

Evelyn knew the name of his gym from the membership card in his wallet, and she strolled up and down the sidewalk in front of it, trying to look casual, stopping for coffee in the restaurant across the road, watching the gym door through the window. When Alika came out, she ran right into him. What a surprise, he said. Of course they just had to go for coffee.

As she sat across from him in the restaurant, trying to force another coffee into her stomach, Evelyn realized Alika wasn't interested in what she was saying. When he said goodbye so easily it almost broke her heart, he made no promise to call. But she remembered where he worked, where he shopped, his home address. He had invited her to all these places by leaving his wallet on her counter.

Evelyn got up from the couch and retrieved her phone from the kitchen. Then she snuggled back under her quilt and dialled Alika's number. She'd been calling him several times a day, since she learned that Wendy was in the hospital, but she was never able to reach him. Tonight it was the same. Wendy's voice on the answering machine. Evelyn hung up. She laid the phone on her belly and closed her eyes, losing herself again in the memory of the happiest days of her life.

One evening, a year ago last spring, Alika and Evelyn ran into each other for the sixth time. Or was it the fifth? Evelyn counted. No. It was the sixth time, and Alika had taken her to a lounge for drinks. And that night he'd taken her home. To his house. She never wanted to leave.

All last June and July, she went to his house every Friday night and spent the weekend, working at making him fall in love with her, at making his house her home. She left her toothbrush, a comb, articles of clothing. She was only waiting for the word from Alika and she'd give up her apartment. She bought a new mat for his bathroom floor and stocked his shelves with her own favourite brand of shampoo. She dug up his garden, even planted those doomed roses.

The roses were cursed. It was because of the roses that Alika met Wendy.

—

Sure, everyone was thinking about me, but no one believed in me anymore. It was unfair.

Evelyn could sense my presence, and I made sure to haunt her as often as I could. It was lonely, though. It seemed unfair that the only person who believed in me was my own murderer. I mean, something had happened to me, at last. Something momentous. All my life I'd been of little consequence, a nobody, a person whose very birth was accidental, a person shifted from family to family at the merest whim of circumstance. And here I was, outrageously wronged, at the very centre of a tragic drama, and nobody even knew about it.

I tried to tell Felix about it, to convince him to give up on questioning Alika, that Alika didn't know anything, and that he should question Evelyn again. But he couldn't hear me. I don't think he believed in the afterlife. He didn't seem to have any religion at all except for the bibliomancy he practised. Every morning he tossed coins on a table top and consulted the I Ching, *though he didn't seem to find any answers in there about my murder. But I could tell he wasn't giving up. He spent a lot of time in his office leafing through the file that held the unfinished story of my death. He'd sigh and rub his head with his hands. He had that look people get when they know there's something they've missed, something that's nagging at them. So I tried to be patient. I was sure he'd figure it out soon, provide some sense of closure to this thing, and Evelyn would be punished. Then I'd finally be able to—well, I wasn't sure what I'd be able to do.*

—

Louise had lost two thousand dollars in the past week, even though she'd played every day. The household account was dangerously low, especially since the mayor had bought himself a handsome new tailor-made pin-striped suit with wide lapels that made him look like a Hollywood gangster.

She needed Bradley Byrnes, but she hadn't been able to reach him for days. So today, though she'd just come from a late afternoon tea at the Chamber of Commerce, and wasn't disguised in the least, she'd taken a chance and come up to his consulting firm.

She waited in the lobby of his building until his receptionist left for the day, and then she took the elevator to the nineteenth floor. He was furious when she walked into his inner office.

"What are you doing here?" He locked the door behind her.

"Why don't you return my calls?"

"I've been busy." Now that the door was locked, he relaxed a bit. He pecked her on the cheek, caressed her hips. "I was going to call you tomorrow."

"Uh huh," said Louise. "Well, I can't wait until tomorrow. I'm in—I'm a little short this month."

"I can fix that," he said. He smiled as he drew his cheque book from his pocket and began to write. "But you remember what we talked about? Last week? I haven't seen any action on that front."

"I know. I talked to him."

"Well, he hasn't done anything. The injunction's still standing. Every day that goes by is money down the drain. And our investors are getting nervous. If they start pulling out—"

"I know, I know." Louise reached for the cheque, but Byrnes held it up above her head. With his other hand, he drew an envelope from his inside pocket.

"It's a simple matter to fix," he said. "A few words in the right places. Give this to your husband, and you'll have nothing to worry about."

Louise took the cheque and the envelope and stuffed them in her straw purse. Nothing to worry about? What the hell did he mean? She placed her hand on the doorknob, planning to flounce out without so much as a kiss goodbye.

But Byrnes grabbed her, hard, by the wrist.

"Not that way," he said. "Take the freight elevator and leave through the loading zone at the back. For God's sake, if anyone sees us together now we're screwed."

As she minced down the alley in her new silk sandals, dodging broken glass and garbage, Louise was fuming. She'd thought she was finished with this damned casino business. She'd thought it was over and done with and Byrnes was in her debt for good. But now he wanted more.

Back at home, she locked herself in her bedroom and opened the envelope. Newspaper clippings. Louise read the first article, something about a trial ten years ago, a trial presided over by the same judge who was in charge of the injunction against demolishing the Walker Theatre. He had given a suspended sentence to a stockbroker accused of embezzling. There were nine articles altogether, spanning twelve years, and in each one the same judge had let somebody off for something.

She hoped Bradley Byrnes knew what he was doing.

—

The garden was overgrown and past all hope now, Noni thought. Only Wendy knew the peculiarities of each plant, each one's special needs. Noni wasn't even sure she knew the difference between a dillweed and a carrot top. It was the first of September, and soon the plants would go to seed, ruining the garden, wasting it. Then Noni would have to phone someone from the yellow pages to come and dig the garden under, but she didn't want to think about that. That was too final. She dipped her spoon into her bowl and tried to eat some of Rosa's pea soup. Maybe she could tempt Alika, who was sitting in front of his own soup, watching it grow cold. But her throat wouldn't open.

Soon it would be time to drive to the hospital again, where they conducted a vigil that filled Noni with dread. Because Wendy wasn't at the hospital. Wendy was lost, and Noni didn't want to look at the body she'd left behind. It lay there, apparently complete, content to rest in its bed almost casually, as though nothing were wrong. Alika spent hours looking at it, and Rosa often talked to it, but Noni hated it. Noni wanted Wendy back, and she often had to leave the building to cry in the parking lot.

Alika did not cry. He didn't even speak of the catastrophe. But Noni noticed that everything slipped through his fingers these days—teacups, pepper shakers, pencils, keys. He had broken most of the wine glasses in the house. Rosa brought him home-made casseroles and fresh salads, but he barely touched them. He was losing weight, growing pale. The scars on his face stood out more prominently than ever.

The doctor had explained several times now, in patient detail, that Wendy might never wake up. The respirator was keeping her lungs and heart functioning. Feeding tubes had been attached to nourish the body, but Wendy's coma, he said, was the deepest he'd ever seen. The possibility of brain damage was high. He suggested gently that the feeding tubes could be removed, if the family decided it was for the best.

"No," Alika said.

—

It hadn't rained once since the night I died, and the garden was beginning to shrivel. The only plants thriving were the weeds. I was worried about the vegetables. They were ninety percent water, after all, didn't Alika know that?

No, I reminded myself, he didn't.

I thought he would miss all the chores I'd performed on a daily basis, but he didn't seem to notice. He didn't seem to care about the things I'd left undone. Did he think that the house would tidy itself? That his drawers would fill up with clean socks of their own accord? Objects lay about the house just as I'd left them. The spoons I was going to clean, more tarnished than ever. The open tin of polish. He hadn't even put the cap back on. He didn't sleep in our bed anymore. Upstairs, the bed remained unmade, the pillow lying carelessly tossed aside since the morning I'd found that stocking. On the dresser, my music box was still open, the way I'd left it, all my personal items jumbled about in plain view.

Worst of all, my library books were overdue.

—

At first, it had given Evelyn some small satisfaction to look up the love spells in the very library where Wendy worked. Evelyn had despised Wendy from the moment she'd heard about her. The day Alika came home with the books about perennial flowers, he'd talked too much about her, mentioned her name too many times, and Evelyn had gone straight down to the library to take a look for herself. Wendy wasn't much to look at. Mouse-brown hair and a sunburned nose. An irritating manner—that dumb, breezy way she gabbed with her coworkers, that dippy way she grinned at the little kids. But in a matter of days she had stolen Alika away from Evelyn. Evelyn was no longer welcome at Alika's house. He was always too "busy" to see her. He told her he didn't think things were "working out" between them.

There was a poetic justice in using the computers at Wendy's branch to steal him back. As she did her research, copying incantations into her notebook, Evelyn kept tabs on Wendy and eavesdropped on her conversations. She knew when Wendy got engaged, when she got married, what Alika had given her for Christmas. She knew all about Wendy, and Wendy had no idea who she was or what she was up to. Or so Evelyn had believed. By the time spring arrived, she was no longer so sure about that.

It was the garden that finally clued Evelyn in to the truth. There was no way any normal person could grow such a garden in that soil, in this city. As she'd watched the seedlings sprout and rise so quickly toward the sun out of that clay-based muck, she realized that Wendy had some sort of unspeakable power. So *that* was why Evelyn's rituals never succeeded. She remembered that once, in the library, when she'd been copying the recipe for a potion from the computer screen, Wendy had walked by, right behind her. At the time, Evelyn had smirked a little. Poor, unsuspecting Wendy! But now she wondered whether Wendy hadn't been reading over her shoulder. Maybe Wendy had launched a counterspell. Wendy was blocking her. Wendy had enchanted Alika somehow, made him immune to Evelyn's magic.

So Evelyn had begun to search the sites for something stronger, something to aim at Wendy, instead of at Alika. That's how, just this spring, a few short months ago, she'd discovered the binding spells.

The instructions for the first binding spell were complicated and required a lot of equipment. It took Evelyn a long time to copy the whole thing off the screen, and it took her several days to collect a black candle, black felt, cotton balls, a metre of red ribbon, and the ingredients for the banishing oil, including pepper oil gum, which Evelyn had never heard of before. In the meantime, she resorted to entering the house when Wendy and Alika went out. She needed certain personal items of Wendy's. And she always left something of her own behind. She became a kind of reverse thief, planting mementos strategically throughout the house. She'd learned from experience that people most desired the things that they had lost, and she wanted to remind Alika that he had lost her.

That first binding spell hadn't worked at all. Everything had gone wrong. Evelyn couldn't obtain any of Wendy's fingernail clippings because, though she had access to the house, and could probably find nail clippings in the trash, she was afraid of collecting Alika's by mistake. So she settled for wisps of hair from Wendy's hairbrush, easily identifiable because of the colour. And instead of pepper oil gum, whatever that was, she used black pepper, chewed-up bubblegum, and a little canola oil. It made a disgusting mixture, and Evelyn could hear Mark laughing at her outside the window as she tried to stir it with a teaspoon. But she didn't allow him to deter her. The June moon was nearly full, and she had to act quickly.

When she had everything assembled, she followed the instructions for making the potion, being cautious while mixing the oils, because the instructions warned that they were volatile. Then she fashioned the felt and cotton poppet that would represent Wendy, stuffed it with the recommended herbs, and sewed it up. She carved Wendy's name into the candle with a thumbtack, anointed the poppet with the binding oil mixture, and began the difficult, somewhat hazardous, ritual, trying not to lose her place as she read aloud from her notebook.

"I bind thee from doing me harm," she said, tying the red ribbon around the poppet's feet. "I bind thee from interfering with my life and my love." She wrapped the arms and the head and finally the entire body of the poppet, so it looked like a little red mummy. The spell went on for several verses, and she had a hard time reading the words while keeping an eye on the candle, trying not to let the flame get too close to the poppet doused in volatile oils.

When at last she'd recited every verse, she held the mummy up to the mirror and visualized all of Wendy's negative energy being reflected back at her. Then she blew out the candle, bundled it together with the poppet in a paper bag, and left the apartment. She carried the package down to the end of the street and buried it on the grounds of the abandoned abattoir.

But it didn't work. If anything, Wendy's power over Alika only increased. It seemed Wendy had created some sort of force field around him, so that Evelyn couldn't arrange to run into him anymore. In mid-August, Wendy took holidays from the library, so that Evelyn was blocked from the house. Then Wendy changed the message on the answering machine so that Evelyn didn't even have the pleasure anymore of hearing Alika's recorded voice before she hung up. Nothing appeared to be binding Wendy from doing Evelyn harm.

Evelyn knew that it must be her own fault. She was an amateur, and the ritual was too advanced for her. Probably the substitution of hair for fingernail clippings had ruined it. Or Evelyn had copied it wrong, skipped some of the words by mistake. Or maybe she hadn't buried the poppet far enough away. She resolved to find some other method, something simple and powerful, something not even a loser like herself could screw up.

—

The mayor was nervous. He understood fully the significance of the newspaper clippings Louise gave him. Or at least he understood that the judge would understand. On the surface, there were no connections linking the items together. They were published articles, articles anyone might have in his possession, about acquittals and suspended sentences. But the mayor knew how these things worked. A story lurked beneath the surface, a pattern that the judge would recognize. The pattern was a hidden threat—sent by whom?

Louise was silent on that point. It was just a little research she'd done, she said. Something she hoped might help the project along. Her behaviour was worrisome, and the mayor tried not to dwell on it. Who had she been talking to? He could ask her, press her on the matter, but it was better if he didn't know. He had learned long ago that the key to staying in power was not knowing things and, with Louise's help, he'd become an expert at it.

Still, he felt he was in over his head. He'd never blackmailed a judge before. He was unsure about the protocol. How should he approach the topic? Jovially, over a glass of whiskey at the Club? Should he make a few jokes about the injunction, man to man, then slip him the envelope of clippings? Hope he'd get the message?

—

As he listened to the uncertain rhythm of Alice's typing, Felix felt a twinge of jealousy, all the more painful because he knew it was irrational. He tried to concentrate on the newspaper spread out before him. Just as he'd predicted, all the letters in today's paper were breathless endorsements of the exciting attractions of the casino. A two-page spread revealed the architect's plans for the new luxury complex, with its skylights and swimming pools and its four-storey arches, like the arches of a Gothic cathedral, that soon would dominate the cityscape. The banality of it all was staggering. Felix felt a wave of nausea pass through him. He folded the paper neatly and carried it into his backyard, where he tossed it into the recycling box.

He stood for a few minutes listening to the rustle of the poplar leaves in the heat. The neighbourhood was quiet, summer languor heavy in the air, hovering low across the yards and gardens, stifling sound. He thought about his neighbour, Wendy Li, and her garden and her fall, and the fact that he still didn't know what had happened to her. Felix and Paul were keeping her file open, but they had no leads.

Restless, he returned to the house and dialled the hospital's information desk to check on Wendy's condition. No change. What if she never woke up? He pictured Wendy lying a few short blocks away, her memory locked inside her, and felt helpless.

He walked down the hall to Alice's room and stood outside her closed door, his knuckles raised to knock. The sound of her typing no longer soothed him. He pictured her fingers as she kneaded the keys, moulding her paper lover into being. He'd seen the way she stacked the pages after she completed each chapter. She held the bundle vertically, tapping the edges of the paper into place, until they were flush. Then she'd lay the new chapter tenderly on top of the growing pile and run her freckled hand across the surface, as if it were a bedsheet she was smoothing.

Felix was beginning to think of the white paper as the surface of a deep lake into which his wife was falling. Far below, a wavering image was forming, a liquid husband who floated among the weeds, holding his arms up toward the light, toward the air, toward Alice, coaxing her to grasp his hand. He was strong, and his voice, made thick by the water, called out for the one who had created him.

—

I was getting fed up with Detective Felix. He was letting himself be sidetracked by every minor detail that crossed his path, while the truth was staring him in the face. All he had to do was return to Evelyn's apartment, perform the most minimal search, and he'd find the evidence he needed. He'd see the photograph of Alika, and he'd surely find the—well, the murder weapon—whatever it was. I was lost, there, as I didn't know how she'd killed me. Whacked me on the head, most likely. Or maybe she had stabbed me. It was hard to tell. The whole event was clouded over in my memory.

I watched while Felix cooked dinner. He was making curry. From scratch. As if he had all the time in the world. Well, you don't, I wanted to scream. A horrible thought struck me. What if Evelyn got away with it? What if she wormed herself back into Alika's life and took my place? It was too terrible to imagine.

Felix, oblivious to this possibility, chopped up everything with excruciating care—onions and garlic and carrots and cauliflower and a big zucchini that looked awfully familiar. What was the matter with him? He had work to do, and instead he was forever cooking dinner and reading newspapers—he was a newspaper addict, this guy—and mooning after his wife. He heated olive oil in a pan and sautéed the onions with the garlic. Then he sprinkled cayenne pepper into a bowl of yogurt and stirred it up. When that cayenne-flavoured yogurt hit the frying pan, a rapturous, pungent aroma suffused the air, and a fierce hunger cut through me.

I felt very keenly all the things that I'd lost. All I had left was my dream of revenge on Evelyn, and now that seemed to be evaporating, too. Here I was, the victim of a gross travesty, the wronged party in a fatal love triangle, and nothing was being done about it. Was it possible that justice was merely an earthly thing? Nothing more than another possession, like a book to read or a bowl of vegetable curry? Would I be forced to surrender it, too, along with everything else?

—

Evelyn's boss telephoned to see if she was feeling better, and she said she was. He sounded sincerely concerned and remarked on the early onset of flu season this year. Evelyn hadn't caught the flu, of course, but she *was* feeling better. She hadn't seen or heard from that detective again. He seemed to have forgotten all about her. Like her boss, he must have believed her lies.

She'd been lying when she said she couldn't remember her activities the night of August twenty-first. It was true she'd been home that evening, but she remembered exactly what she'd been doing. It was the day after she'd found the new binding spell. When she first came across it, on a new magic web site, she'd been delighted. It was elegant and clean. She had all the necessary materials right in her apartment, and she resolved to cast the spell right away. But back at home, she had second thoughts. Even though the spell seemed simple, she didn't want to take any chances. She would practise, test it out on someone else first. Now, who else was sapping her energy? Who was else was harassing her, refusing to leave her alone, making her life miserable?

She drew a picture of a mosquito on a piece of paper, copying it from her old biology textbook. She folded the paper three times, tied it up with black thread, and put it in an old marmalade jar full of water. She repeated the words of the spell, which were eloquently sparse and easy to remember, even a little silly: "Do as I please, stay there and freeze." Then she put the marmalade jar in the freezer compartment of her fridge.

That very night, the fogging trucks drove down her back lane and up her front street, spraying the neighbourhood with insecticide. In the morning, Evelyn had a dry, sore throat and a headache. But when she stood outside and offered her bare arms up to be bitten, only one mosquito appeared. It flew toward her, weaving wildly as though drunk, then fell dead at her feet. There was not another one in sight. The courtyard outside her apartment block was mosquito-free.

When she opened the freezer again, she saw that the ice had expanded, cracking the glass. She wrapped the broken jar in newspaper and threw it in the garbage. Searching among her cupboards, she found a plastic yogurt cup with a lid. She planned to use it that very night, when the timing would be most fortuitous. That evening, August twenty-first, a full moon would rise, lending its womanly powers to any spell cast beneath its light. Evelyn hurried home from her late shift at the convenience store. She lit a few candles, just to set the right atmosphere, get herself into the mood. Then she ripped a scrap of paper from her notebook and wrote Wendy's name on it carefully, in blue ink. She placed the scrap in the yogurt cup, filled it with water and snapped on the lid. At midnight, she recited the magic sentence as she placed it in the freezer behind the vanilla ice cream. Take that!

5

BEFORE COMPLETION

At night, while the world of the living slept, I could hear the dead whispering, calling me, coaxing me toward them. At these times, I took shelter in the library. I feared their siren songs, feared my own despair, the great temptation to surrender. And books were the only refuge I had ever known from such strange longings.

I'd always wanted to be all alone in the library at night, and now I could be. During the bustle of the day, surrounded by books that I didn't have time to read, I'd often imagined sneaking in after hours, stealing the luxury of time. I had time now, in abundance.

The dark rows of shelves were beautiful under the dim night lighting, as I'd always imagined they would be, tall monuments, like rows of gravestones in a cemetery. I'd always thought that if I could get in at night, I'd finally have a chance to explore the library thoroughly, to browse through history, *biography, cookbooks, atlases. But now that I was here, I found myself drawn back to the children's section, to the bulletin board that should have been changed last week, to my own desk, my unfinished paperwork.*

I saw all the tasks that needed to be done. The unshelved volumes in the back room, where no child could ever find them. A box of shiny new animal books that hadn't yet been catalogued. A forgotten stack of paperbacks about the weather, left over from the display we'd made in spring, when we studied the wind and made those kites.

I wandered into the fiction section. My favourite shelf was the one with the Children's Classics, the hardcover collection. The broad spines of the books were blue, green, deep chocolate brown, and ruby red, the titles stamped in golden, Gothic script: Treasure Island, Alice in Wonderland, Heidi, Anne of Green Gables, Peter Pan.

Peter Pan! *I would have given anything to open that volume and look at the watercolour illustrations, read that story again. To get past the covers to those thick, creamy pages, those letters, words. Sometimes I thought this was the very worst part of it all. The saddest. The least bearable.*

———

When Noni drove Alika home from the hospital that evening, Evelyn was standing in the shadow of the lilac bush. As she watched him emerge from his sister's car, she stepped behind the branches, so that Noni wouldn't see her. Noni hated Evelyn. It must have been Noni who'd told that detective about her. Evelyn had been terrified for days, but now that she'd calmed down, she reasoned that

Noni had probably sent the detective to her door just to harass her. He probably didn't suspect her at all. He hadn't even looked in her freezer. She was starting to relax. She was going to get away with it. She could barely believe her own power.

She watched as Alika searched his pockets, looking for his keys. He entered the house and turned on the kitchen light. Evelyn moved into the backyard, so she could see him through the window. She noted that Wendy's garden was full of weeds. So, Wendy was truly gone. She was lying in the hospital, defeated, and Alika was alone, or almost alone. Evelyn's things lay strewn throughout the house, unseen but surely emitting their scent, beckoning him.

She watched Alika's silhouette pace from the table to the sink and back again. He seemed smaller, somehow, but Evelyn didn't want to think about that. She thought instead about the curtains in the window, how sheer they were. Wendy had bought them. Evelyn would never choose curtains like that. She wouldn't want anyone lurking around, spying on her. No. If Evelyn moved in with Alika, she'd buy thick curtains, dark ones, and she'd change the kitchen bulb to a lower wattage. Better yet, they'd dine by candlelight.

Alika sat at the table in his usual chair and looked across at Wendy's empty place. He leaned his elbows on the table and rested his head in his hands. For the past year, Evelyn had watched him through this window with a keen jealousy, adrenaline coursing through her bloodstream. It had been a painful year. But it was over now. Evelyn had won. So why didn't she feel like celebrating?

Alika began to pace again. His shoulders, once so broad and upright, sagged. Evelyn felt a soft pang rush through her body. She didn't recognize this feeling right away, but gradually, as she stood there among the mosquitoes, with the tall blades of the uncut lawn tickling her bare legs, she realized that it was pity.

—

Alice was in her study, conversing leisurely with her daemon lover. She would tap out a five- or six-letter word and then pause, as though waiting for him to answer. The closer she came to the end of the book, Felix thought, the more slowly she wrote. She was delaying, lingering, loitering sensuously. Unwilling to depart.

Felix put on his jacket and slipped quietly out the front door. He had taken to walking down to the hospital on those evenings when Alice was writing. He'd tell the nurses that he wanted to interview Wendy Li, and the nurses always told him she was still unconscious. But Felix would sit beside her bed and speak to her anyway, asking her questions and, lately, telling her things. About his cooking and Alice's book, and the goings-on in the neighbourhood.

Tonight, he hesitated on the threshold of her room, uncertain whether to enter. Wendy's husband was there, pacing the floor in front of the window. The hospital lights were dimmed at night, and the dark window revealed nothing except a reflection of the cold, white room, the sterile machinery, their own two bodies standing there, useless and bereft. Felix coughed and Alika looked up. The two men acknowledged each other without speaking.

Felix had spoken to the doctor. He knew it was foolish to hope for a recovery, that the machines Alika refused to turn off were only delaying, only prolonging, his loss. And yet at times it seemed to Felix that it might be possible to reach through and touch Wendy Li on the other side, the way he had once reached through the dark waters of the lake and retrieved that drowning boy. Pulled him by the hair up into the oxygen and returned him to his parents. Whole. A miracle, Alice had called it. Maybe it was.

"Any change?" Felix asked.

Alika shook his head. He turned away and faced the window, straining his eyes against the black glass, as though trying to penetrate the film that lay across the surface of things.

—

Alika was still unaware of me. I followed him as he forced himself to dress and eat and drive to and from the hospital. I worried that he hadn't watered the garden. He hadn't even entered it, and the weeds were taking over. A Canadian thistle had sprouted among the cabbages and was thriving—four feet tall, blooming bristly purple flowers full of bumblebees.

At night, Alika collapsed onto the living room couch without bothering to shower. I stayed close and listened to him breathe, longing to hold him, to feel the movement of his lungs, his heartbeat. I often used to suffer from insomnia over some trivial problem—the library budget cuts or one of Evelyn's hairpins. I'd lie awake and press my ear to his chest and feel his beating heart reverberating through his body and through mine. I hadn't even minded that he snored. I was glad to remember that. I'd have been ashamed, now that I was dead, to think I'd ever been so petty.

I left my sleeping husband and wandered out to the garden. It was dark now, and the bees had returned to their hive, but the mosquitoes were congregating. A new swarm had hatched in the bird bath, and they were hungry, looking for blood. Their high-pitched whining surrounded and enclosed me, and it was strangely comforting.

The night was muggy and dark under the new moon, and I longed for company. I rose with the mosquitoes into the air that was thick with the dusky smell of tomato plants— Alika should have been picking those tomatoes—over the lilac bushes and down the lane to the river bank, where they would feed on crows and sleeping sparrows. They didn't feed on me. I floated in the swarm with impunity, as if I were one of them, free at last of their itches and stings.

—

It was bad luck to voice any negative thoughts about Wendy, Rosa scolded Noni. It was tempting the gods.

"You've got it backwards, Mum," Noni said. "It's hubris that tempts the gods, over-confidence."

Rosa eyed her suspiciously. "Is that what they taught you in college?"

"As a matter of fact, yes," Noni said. "But all I'm saying is that we should be prepared. The doctor says—"

"The doctor!" Rosa said. "I suppose he went to college, too!"

"I certainly hope so." Noni sighed. She was exhausted. She didn't know anymore what caused good luck and what caused bad luck. It seemed to her that a wild undercurrent of total randomness snaked and bucked beneath their everyday lives. And what use was luck now? According to the doctor, the worst thing that could possibly happen had already happened.

Rosa insisted that she'd have some intimation if Wendy was going to die, and Noni had always trusted in her mother's premonitions before. But now it seemed to Noni that if there was a veil between the present and the future, it raised and lowered itself at meaningless intervals, revealing the most inconsequential things, like the arrival of the garbage truck, and concealing the answers to crucial questions, as if it didn't understand, or care anymore, about the difference between life and death.

—

The voices of the dead grew more persuasive. I didn't try to make out the words. I wasn't even sure if they were speaking English, but it didn't matter. Their tone said everything. It was seductive, persistent, promising. I wondered sometimes if I was supposed to answer. But I'd never known anyone who'd died, and I didn't know how to talk to them. What would I say?

Would I have to account for myself, the way Mrs. Keller always said I would? And what could I really say about my life, anyway? What had I accomplished? It occurred to me I'd barely skimmed the surface of the earth while I was there. I swept and the dust came back. I weeded and the weeds came back. I cooked dinners and people ate them. Even my marriage, which I'd thought meant an end to being alone, was done and undone in a twinkling. I'd loved Alika for one entire year and yet I scarcely knew him.

—

Gradually, Evelyn was starting to suspect that the freezer binding spell had failed. Even though Wendy was lying there as good as dead, none of the bad effects of her power were diminishing. If anything, Evelyn's troubles had only increased. Alika still paid no attention to her. When she called, he barely mumbled into the receiver at her, two or three words at a time, before he hung up. He always said he wanted to keep the line free. And Evelyn was developing a guilty conscience. Her remorse—or some kind of restless presence—hounded her at night and drove her from her bed to see what she could see through Alika's curtains. But instead of enjoying the fact that he was all alone at last, instead of revelling in her victory, Evelyn had begun to worry about him. She worried about herself, too. Why did she bother sneaking around like this? Alika didn't even know she was alive. One afternoon, on her way to work, she decided it was time to show herself in daylight.

There was Alika on the front steps, fiddling with some red cloth and sticks of wood.

"Hi," Evelyn said.

He looked up briefly. "Hi, Evelyn."

"What are you doing?"

"I'm fixing Wendy's kite," he said.

"Oh. Wendy's better, then?"

"She will be." He kept his head low, eyes averted, concentrating on a thin stick of balsa wood.

No matter what Evelyn said, Alika answered only in short syllables. He kept his focus on the kite. Here she was, right in front of him, free and available, his for the taking, and he couldn't even see her. Wendy was completely unavailable, thanks to Evelyn, but this had only made her more desirable. Alika was living inside a house chock full of Wendy's things. Evelyn's meagre offerings—a single stocking, a comb—didn't stand a chance against the arsenal of Wendy's worldly possessions, against her underwear, against that kite. Evelyn said goodbye as casually as she could and turned away, tears stinging her eyes.

The freezer binding spell had worked all right. It had worked too well. It had backfired, and now Alika was under Wendy's power more than ever before. Evelyn should have seen the risks. The spell wasn't specific enough. It prevented Wendy from doing Evelyn harm, but it also prevented her from doing anything else.

Now, Wendy would never nag Alika or neglect him or become unfaithful. She would never grow fat and boring, like the wives the firemen complained of. She wouldn't ever age. Alika would always remember her the way she was the day that Evelyn had cast the spell on her—young and healthy, and in love, surrounded by morning glory in full bloom.

Wendy had become immortal.

—

It was many years since Rosa had worked in a garden. Since the car accident, her back had been weak, prone to slipped disks and bouts of sciatica. But if she didn't do something soon, all of Wendy's work would be in vain. Wendy would be appalled, when she came home, to see her garden like this. Rosa had finally watered it yesterday, but water wasn't enough. Even if the rains came, the vegetation would rot. The lettuce and cabbage leaves would grow slimy and full of slugs. She fingered the tangle of yellow beans that had dried out and were now inedible. Yes, something needed to be done. She retrieved some tools from the shed and stood for a few minutes, trying to decide where to begin.

Rosa dragged a hoe across the weeds between the potatoes. The weeds were tall and growing strong. Hundreds of baby elm trees had sprouted since Wendy's fall, and their little stems were already tough and woody. Rosa had to use the trowel to dig them out. Her back began to ache.

"Alika! Look!" Noni stood at the kitchen door, pointing. Alika looked up and saw his mother in the garden, working.

"Mum, you'll hurt your back," Noni called.

Rosa didn't answer. She waded through the crabgrass into the spreading tomato plants, picking tomatoes as she went, until her pail was full. She pulled up three enormous onions and placed them on top, careful not to bruise the delicate skin of the tomatoes, which were overripe. Then she forged her way through a veritable hedge of thistles into the cabbage patch. What had Wendy done to these plants to make them grow so large? Rosa remembered her mother's stock answer to any questions about where babies came from: "*Je t'ai trouvée en-dessous d'un chou.*" I found you under a cabbage. Well, Wendy's cabbages were easily big enough to conceal a baby. Rosa stooped and lifted a leaf, inspecting the underside for slugs. The leaf was clean and dry. No slugs. And no babies. But she did find, snug up against the stem of the cabbage, a 35-millimetre automatic camera, one of Alika's cameras. How did that get there? Rosa tucked it safely into her apron pocket. She wondered whether her son was losing his mind.

—

In the darkroom, Alika submerged a set of prints in a tray of developing fluid. Noni often liked to watch this process, and today she was curious about the results. When he'd opened the camera Rosa had found in the garden, he'd discovered a roll of film. He doubted it would be any good, but Rosa insisted he try to develop it. The work would be good for him, she said. It would keep him in practice for when he went back to the studio. She had lately decided that work would be good for all of them, especially work that they did together. She went to Noni's apartment and did laundry while Noni finished making the tangerine dress she'd neglected and caught up on the alterations. At Alika's house, Rosa assigned a number of tasks, washing and mending Wendy's clothing, fixing her kite. Tomorrow, they were all supposed to start canning the pumpkins. But creative work, Rosa said, was best of all. It would ease Alika's mind. As in most things these days, Rosa had been wrong about that. Alika was as gaunt and silent as ever.

Noni stood behind her brother and placed a hand on his shoulder as she watched the transformation in the developing tray. An image started to lift to the surface of the floating paper. At first, the patterns were arbitrary, stray threads of darkness gathering where the absence of light had brushed the surface of the film and disappeared. Then Noni could make out a set of teeth, a pair of eyes—a man's face. And there was a woman beside him.

"Who are these people?" she asked.

Alika shook his head. "I don't know," he said. "But I'm going to find out."

—

I'd never watched Alika in his darkroom before. I'd never seen him measuring chemicals, shaking containers so carefully, timing things. I knew he went into the darkroom and emerged with photographs, but I'd never thought about how he made it happen.

Alika had always seemed to me so mysteriously dense that I hadn't thought it possible to know him. Maybe I'd preferred not to know him. I'd been able to spend a lot of time imagining the murky depths of his being. When he stared blankly at the ceiling or the sky or the blades of grass, I'd thought of him as hopelessly impractical, sweetly lost without my guidance. But he wasn't lost. He was looking at things.

I remembered the stack of pictures he'd taken of those autumn leaves, their fragile veins, the sunlight bleeding through their golden skins like fire. That was what he'd seen, what he'd brought to light here in the darkness.

—

On the rare occasions when Alice left her work to go out, Felix had taken to reading her manuscript compulsively. He felt guilty about it, but he couldn't stop himself. Alice didn't end the story with the solving of the crime, or even with a brief account of what happened to the principal characters. She went on and on, telling the story of Felix's convalescence, her slow, deliberate courtship of him.

No wonder she couldn't meet her deadline. Alice's manuscript had long ago ceased to be a true-crime book and was becoming a romance novel. She recounted her visits to the hospital after Felix had been wounded, the meals she'd brought for him, the time she cut his hair, the day he first walked down the corridor, leaning on her arm. Felix couldn't help grinning when he came across the account of their first night together. He'd forgotten that episode in the hospital bathroom, with the bubble bath.

He'd forgotten a lot, he realized, as he turned the pages. He read every detail of their wedding and reception, their breathless, laughing dash through the rain to the car and the ride back to this house. They were supposed to drive up to the lake for their honeymoon, but there had been a wild thunderstorm that night, and they'd come here instead, to their new home, even though they hadn't finished moving in yet. When the storm took down the electric lines, and all the lights on the street went out, they discovered they had no candles. She'd been frightened, and he remembered how she'd clung to him in bed, tightening her grip each time the lightning flashed. To soothe her, Felix had told stories all night long. He was surprised to see that she remembered every story he'd told, for he himself had long forgotten them. She described the sound of Felix's voice in the darkness, gentle and low, a sound she could sleep inside of. And now she was returning the favour, Felix thought. The pages she'd written were full of blooming tenderness, and lust. For Felix, or for this other Felix who was beginning, he recognized with a shock, to resemble himself.

———

My sister- and mother-in-law embraced each other in the doorway of my house, and then they parted. Noni carried my library books to her car, and Rosa returned to the garden with a pair of scissors to cut the oregano for drying. They were taking care of things, erasing the signs of my absence, replacing me.

The oregano had flowered, and Rosa began by cutting the pale, amethyst blooms from the tops of the stalks, letting them fall to the ground in soft heaps. The poppy seeds had been scattered, the pumpkins harvested. The bird bath had been freshly filled, and a breeze rippled the surface of its water.

———

When Felix saw Alika standing on his front porch, he was frightened. Had Wendy passed away at last? He sent up a brief prayer as he opened the door.

"I have something to show you," Alika said.

Felix had never seen him so animated before. He was agitated about something, but it wasn't Wendy's death. He was holding a large envelope under his arm.

"Come in." Felix led the way to the kitchen, poured two cups of tea, and told Alika to sit.

"I found my camera," Alika said. He opened the envelope and spilled photographs onto the kitchen table. "And these were in it. Look."

Felix looked. He recognized the event—The Concerned Citizens' protest against the new casino. The event that had never appeared in the newspaper. The citizens had marched through downtown and defiantly crossed the street at Portage and Main, where pedestrian traffic was forbidden. The photos had been taken at City Hall, at the rally after the march. People were jostling each other, trying to get closer to the camera. They carried hand-lettered signs. "Don't gamble with our future." "The wages of sin is death." "Hospitals, not Casinos!"

There was the mayor, trying to maintain his dignity before the crowd of hecklers. There was the mayor's wife, slipping into City Hall. She was trying to conceal her face with a newspaper, but Felix recognized her. He'd seen her that day in that mauve dress and matching shoes, the straw purse like a beach bag that she carried in the summertime. Felix had been standing just inside the glass doors of the City Hall as she'd slipped past, murmuring something about a migraine, her need to find a cool place to lie down. Yes. In the next photograph, Felix could see the back of his own head, and his own arm holding the door open for her.

"I was there that day," Felix said.

"It was the day Wendy got hurt."

Felix looked up sharply. That was true.

Alika nodded. "I took these pictures, took my camera home that afternoon, but never took the film out. I didn't have time. I had to get to Gino's. I was working the late shift. And when I got home—"

"I know."

"So I never realized my camera was missing until my mother found it the other day. When I developed the film, and saw what I had, I thought I'd better show you right away."

Felix wondered where all of this was going. "Your camera went missing?"

"Yeah—since the night Wendy fell. But I never knew— I never looked for it. And then my mother found it."

"Where?"

Alika was distracted, searching for a particular picture. "*En-dessous d'un chou*," he said.

"What?"

"In the garden, under a cabbage. Look at this one."

Felix looked closely. City Hall from the outside. He recognized the windows of the boardroom, where the mayor's wife had been resting in the darkness. But there was a light on in the window.

"Then I used the zoom," Alika said. He handed Felix the next shot, a close-up. Through the boardroom window, Felix could clearly see a man kissing a woman.

A woman with a straw hat and purse. The mayor's wife.

"What else have you got?" he asked.

Alika pushed the stack across the table.

Felix flipped through every shot. In one, a man was exiting the building from the back, a man looking straight at the photographer. Someone very small and slim. Marty Smith. The kid he'd seen that morning in Wendy's bushes. Not very far from the cabbages.

—

Martin Dexter Smith gave Felix the fastest, most complete confession he'd heard in his entire career. The kid seemed relieved to be arrested, and was all too eager to paint himself as a victim. He simply caved, and the whole ugly story came out.

Marty worked as a courier and file clerk for his mother's boss, Bradley Byrnes of Byrnes Consulting, who had taken Marty under his wing and promised him a steady job as long as he remained discreet. It was Byrnes who was kissing the mayor's wife. He'd seen Alika snapping shots and sent Marty after him to get the film. Marty had bungled this simple job badly. He'd followed Alika home and waited until he left again, without the camera. Then Marty drove his own car several blocks away before returning on foot. He knocked on the door, to make sure no one was home. Then he entered the unlocked house, looking for the camera, which he'd found, very quickly, upstairs in a darkroom.

Felix winced at the pride in Marty's voice.

The sorry tale continued. As Marty had hurried down the hallway with his find, a door suddenly opened, right in front of him, and Wendy Li had appeared out of nowhere. In his rush to get past her, to get out of the house, he'd knocked her over. He didn't mean to push her down the stairs. He fell, too, he hastened to add. He'd have probably been killed, if he hadn't landed on top of her.

"What did you do then?" Felix asked.

"What do you think I did? I ran!"

"Through the garden."

"Yeah! I went out through the back and I tripped—all those plants and stuff—and I dropped the thing—the camera. It must have rolled. I couldn't find it anywhere."

"So you came back the next morning."

"Yeah. But you were there. Then once you'd seen me I stayed the hell away."

"Byrnes didn't ask you for the film?"

"I told him I destroyed it."

Felix rubbed his aching head. "And all of this just so Byrnes could cover up his affair with Louise Douglas."

"Well," said Marty, slyly, "I don't think it was just the affair."

—

The mayor's wife checked herself into a treatment centre for problem gamblers, to avoid the growing scandal. The centre was newly renovated, and though it was a very old building, it was modern inside. It used to be a school for girls, the director told her. St. Bernadette's.

"I'd give you a tour," the director said, "but we have Group in five minutes."

"Group?" said Louise.

"You'll see."

Group turned out to be an embarrassment, with women standing up and telling the most dreadful stories about the messes they got into. Louise had nothing in common with any of them. Some of them had become thieves to support their habit, and Louise took careful note of those ones, planning to avoid them at the dinner table.

Louise hadn't expected to find any friends at the centre. She'd always kept to herself. But there was one decent sort there, a woman named Betty, a housewife and mother, like herself. Betty seemed to like Louise, and as the days went by, Louise found herself chatting, even laughing sometimes, with Betty. There was also a very respectable volunteer named Mrs. Kowalski, who sat in the lounge in the evenings, knitting and dispensing advice to the residents. But she wouldn't play cards.

Cards were not allowed in the centre. No Monopoly, no games of chance of any sort. Betty tried to persuade Mrs. Kowalski to bring some checkers, arguing that checkers was a game of skill, but Mrs. Kowalski merely smiled and brought out the jigsaw puzzles.

"I'll bet I can finish mine before you finish yours," Betty said.

DISPERSION

So.

I wasn't at the centre of this story after all.

I was way off on the periphery, and I didn't like it. When I heard Felix explaining to my family what had happened, I didn't believe him at first. I'd wanted it all to mean something, my death, my so-called murder. I'd thought it meant I was beloved, envied, wronged, and soon to be avenged.

But when I heard all the evidence, I realized it was indisputable. I wasn't the victim of passion at all, but merely of panic, clumsiness. Sure, I'd been wronged. I had even been murdered, in a technical sort of way. But it was all so impersonal. Incidental. My death, like my birth, had been a slip-up. It was humiliating.

There was another point as well. Along with everything else, I would have to give up my haunting of Evelyn. I would miss her sorely. For I'd been attached to her, as deeply as I'd been attached to anything else on earth.

I couldn't resist a last visit to her apartment. There she was, reading the newspaper and eating a snack. She bit daintily into a piece of green apple. The apple looked crisp and cold, its white flesh cut into fresh slices, fanned out on a blue plate beside a triangle of soft cheese. And she was drinking a yellow wine that sparkled in its glass. But as I watched her drink, I realized I didn't begrudge her this pleasure. I wasn't at all thirsty.

All I could think of was the word: thirsty. *Whatever had it meant?*

—

Felix took home the growing file on Marty Smith. He hated to bring police work home, feeling it contaminated the house, and ordinarily he didn't. But today he'd come home early at Alice's request. She had something to tell him, she'd said, but she wasn't home yet. She'd left a note promising her swift return from the grocery store. Some last-minute item.

Marty's file was pathetic, as Felix had known it would be. Marty had suffered a hard childhood. He had a juvenile record for shoplifting, uttering threats, and attempted extortion. He'd learned early how to trade in information. He'd already given Felix a lot of details about errands he'd run for Byrnes, and hinted that there was "a lot more where that came from." Felix didn't know what the "lot more" was, but he expected to hear all about it when the prosecutor sat down to deal with Marty's lawyer.

Felix closed the file, depressed by its contents. Poppy was rubbing against his leg, begging for a treat, and he stood up to get her a biscuit. He locked the file in his briefcase, out of sight. As he followed Poppy to the kitchen, Felix stopped once again to marvel at the dining room. Fresh flowers, linen napkins, candlesticks. It made him nervous. Whatever Alice was going to tell him, it must be important.

—

Evelyn read the unfolding news stories with awe and disappointment. And a sense of relief that came as a surprise to her. She was not the cause of Wendy's coma. She was not the cause of anything, she realized. And she should have known it. She had never, in her whole life, made anything happen at all.

This petty thief, this wretched, lamentable Martin Dexter Smith, had made something happen. He had created an uproar in the city, an outrage at City Hall, front page headlines for three days running.

Yet he'd done it all by mistake, if Evelyn understood correctly. With a single stumble, he had ruined his boss and the mayor's wife and even the mayor himself, though the mayor denied all knowledge, ridiculed the accusations. Evelyn read the accusations—blackmail, influence peddling, kickbacks, conflict of interest. She didn't understand all those terms very clearly, but she got the general idea. These people had tried to fix the odds behind the scenes, pulling strings as if they were puppeteers. But powerful as they were, they'd been no match for Smith.

Maybe it wasn't possible to control anything with certainty.

Evelyn felt the familiar stab of fear this thought had always brought her. But instead of jumping up and doing something to contain it, she let it spread throughout her body, let it split her wide open. It was worse than she'd ever imagined, like a surgeon's hacksaw breaking her breast bone in two. But this time she lay there and took it.

—

Felix went to visit Louise Douglas at the treatment centre, hoping to convince her to testify against Byrnes, so that the prosecution wouldn't rest solely on Marty's credibility. Louise was in Group, so Felix sat down in the lounge to wait until she filed in, along with five other women, all of them looking tired and dissatisfied.

Louise admitted to her affair. But that was as far as she'd go.

"Look," she said to Felix. "I admit I made mistakes. I had a problem. But I'm moving forward now, I'm getting help."

As he listened, Felix could see the story of her innocence taking shape, becoming smoother each time she rehearsed it. Becoming believable, becoming a sure thing. Because Louise Douglas, despite the games of chance she played, wasn't a person who believed in taking chances.

He looked around the lounge. Six sad, ordinary women. Gamblers. But probably none of them believed in taking chances. Who would throw the dice, believing that the outcome would be arbitrary? No one. These women must have believed that a deep and unseen justice structured the world, that it ordered the outcome of their games. Maybe they still believed it. Like everybody else, they had been robbed, and they expected someday everything would be restored to them. They deserved it. And suddenly Felix had a vision. He was struck by the certain knowledge that this strong, abiding faith was everywhere, that it would swell forth from the bowels of the city and propel the great casino plans to victory. The clouds of scandal would eventually disperse, and he could see the casino rising high above the city, its glass and emerald tower gleaming on the skyline like a beacon.

———

Evelyn was exhausted, emptied out from sobbing. And her lungs ached. She'd always thought that if she gave in like that, she would die from the pain. But here she was, eating another apple. The grieving had made her hungry. She'd keened for her mother, her father, her brother who she couldn't save, who she couldn't bring back completely. She wasn't capable of bringing anybody back. It was a harsh truth, and it still hurt.

But if she couldn't bring anyone back, she thought now, then maybe she wasn't responsible for losing them in the first place.

She looked at the poster on her wall, the cool, clear stream pouring down the mountainside. If she wanted to want something, she thought, she might as well want something she could have.

———

Alice admitted that she couldn't finish the book because she didn't want their story to end, and Felix promised her that it never would. Especially not now that they were going to have a baby. No wonder she was sleeping so much, he said.

"Do you believe in reincarnation?" Alice asked him. "Do you think our baby has an old soul?"

Felix looked up from his newspaper, where he was reading about a proposal for a new arena. He smiled. "I don't know," he said.

"I do," Alice said. "I believe we're all, well, rotating, sort of, on a giant wheel. We go around and around, getting on and off here and there."

"So you believe in karma, then?"

"No. Not exactly," she said. "It's more like, I don't know, like a giant roulette wheel."

Felix laughed. "Do we have any choice when we get on and off?"

"Yes, I think we do," Alice said.

"You mean we decide when to die?"

"Maybe." She stroked her belly. "But I was thinking, more, you know—that we decide when to live, to come to earth."

"You mean we chose to be here?"

"I did," Alice told him. "I chose to be right here. With you." She moved closer and placed her hand in his.

Felix didn't know anymore what he believed in terms of chance and the randomness of his own life, the lives of others. But he wasn't stupid. He knew he was a lucky man.

—

Evelyn gave her notice at the convenience store and asked for a letter of reference. She gave away her furniture to a women's shelter. She had stayed up all night packing and now it was nearly dawn. The only chore left was to finish cleaning the kitchen before she called a taxi to take her to the bus depot.

She unplugged the fridge and set about clearing its contents, tossing out shrivelled lemons and leftover pizza. She took the ice cream out of the freezer and saw the yogurt cup. She'd forgotten it there when she stopped believing in the spell. It seemed irrelevant now. She set it on the counter. Then she stood at the sink, eating every last spoonful of French Vanilla out of the carton. She mopped the floor lightly one last time and then surveyed her empty apartment. She had no one to say goodbye to.

She thought about walking past Alika's house, knocking on his door, telling Alika that she forgave him. She decided that wasn't a good idea. Still, she felt the urge to make some final gesture. And she had the time. She picked up the yogurt container. Clear, tiny beads of condensation were forming on its plastic sides.

When the Greyhoud bus pulled out of the depot, the sun was just beginning to rise. Evelyn arranged a pillow under her head and settled in to enjoy the ride. Outside the window of the bus, the faint outline of her brother moved his hands through the air, practising some conjuring trick. What was it he was trying to do? Evelyn smiled. Mark had always wanted to become invisible. Maybe if she let him go, he'd finally learn to disappear.

—

When Rosa saw the running shoe on Alika's kitchen table, she turned pale.

"Noni! What are you thinking?"

Noni entered the kitchen. "What?"

"This!" Rosa plucked the offending runner from the table and shook it at her daughter. "A shoe! On the table! In this house of all houses!"

"Oh, Mum," Noni said. "I just laid it there for a second."

"A second is all it takes for bad luck to enter the house. I've told you that."

Noni took her shoe and walked out of the kitchen, straight down the hall and out the front door. She stood on the steps, aware that it was a glorious autumn morning, but unable to enjoy it. Rosa was driving her crazy lately with her rules and esoteric codes. She seemed to believe that she was the only one who could read the world, decipher its secret injunctions, keep them all safe. Noni didn't believe she'd ever feel safe again, no matter how careful she was about where she put her shoes.

Rosa followed her out onto the steps. "Alika's up," she said. "Come in and have coffee. We'll burn some sage and purify the house."

Noni whirled around. "Will you stop it? Honestly, do you really think it makes any difference what we burn, or what we spill, or whether or not we break a mirror?"

"Of course it does."

"Well, look what happened to Wendy," Noni cried. "Wendy didn't do anything. Look what happened to Alika. What did he ever do to deserve this?"

"Maybe they did something and they don't know it," Rosa said thoughtfully. "They're careless sometimes. But from you—" Rosa pointed at the runner Noni was holding. "I didn't expect this from you."

Noni threw the runner onto the grass. "I suppose that's bad luck, too," she said. "Throwing one shoe—one left shoe. Oh! And look at that—maple seeds on the lawn. Isn't that bad luck? And look, a bottle cap on the sidewalk. And this—what's this?" She reached down and picked up a plastic container from the bottom step. "A yogurt cup. That's bad luck for sure—a yogurt cup on your front steps. That spells certain doom!"

Rosa turned away. "I don't know what's the matter with you," she said as she went back inside.

But Noni was staring at the cup. "It's frozen," she said. "How could that be?"

She pried off the lid and looked inside. Nothing but white ice, with a scrap of something embedded within it. Noni squeezed the container until the ice began to crack, then she drew out the scrap. Just a torn piece of paper with a smudge of blue ink across it. She sighed. She didn't even want to try to understand this one.

Alika opened the door and said, "Mum says to come to breakfast."

"I know," said Noni. "I owe her an apology." She thrust the cold container into his hand and entered the house.

Alika barely glanced at it. A clutch of floating silver maple seeds had caught his eye. It touched down on his open palm, delicate and light. He closed his fingers around it for a moment, then opened them and let it blow away.

Rosa called from inside. "Alika! The coffee's ready."

But Alika wasn't listening. He was watching the silver maple. A gust of wind lifted its branches, pulling hundreds of white seeds from its limbs at once. He watched them coasting through the air, drifting across the lawns of the neighbourhood.

Warmed by his hand, the ice in the yogurt cup began to melt.

—

Alika sipped his coffee, grimaced, and decided to add sugar. He could never remember that he wanted sugar until he tasted the coffee and found it bitter. It was the same with milk in his cereal. Every time he lifted a spoonful of cereal to his lips, he was surprised to find it dry, lacking. He was a man with too many expectations. I guessed he wasn't stupid, after all. He was extraordinarily hopeful.

He seemed to be eating, finally, but it was hard to tell. The whole scene before me was disintegrating. Alika's face was smudged, his movements blurred, or perhaps it was my own vision that was failing. For a long time now my vision had been failing. My thoughts were disconnected, thinning out across the room, becoming watery. Nothing was holding together.

Alika lifted his spoon and suddenly, for a second, I could see the dull, unpolished silver, just as though it were real, and then everything began to pull apart as easily as cotton candy. The kitchen stretched wide, it wavered. And just before it all dissolved, I felt the insides of my body turning outward, entering everything.

—

Felix didn't know why he went to visit Wendy Li again. He hardly knew her as a neighbour, and her case was solved. But he went. Today she seemed the same as ever. Felix sat down beside the bed and said, "Hello there."

He didn't know whether she could hear him or even, if she could, whether he should tell her all the things he told her when he sat beside her bed. He felt a little guilty about telling her the story of Marty Smith the other day. Maybe that wasn't the kind of thing you wanted to hear when you were in a coma. So today he kept it light. He told her about Alice and the baby, about the silver maple at home, dispensing its seeds until they carpeted St. Catherine Street like early snow.

A faint movement of the muscles on Wendy's cheek startled him. He wasn't sure, but he thought he saw the eyelids flicker.

"Wendy?" Felix took her hand in his and squeezed gently. He thought he felt a pressure in return.

"Nurse?" Felix called. "Nurse!" He tried to rise, but Wendy's white hand had gripped his own and would not let go. He stared at her face. Her features were still and pale, impassive. But her grip was so strong that he couldn't wriggle his fingers free. He tried again to call a nurse, but his throat had gone dry.

And then Felix saw the eyes open completely. The blue-green eyes. Looking right at him.

—

Rosa was rolling out dough for a pie crust and Noni was patching a rip in a pair of blue jeans. Alika sat silently, doing nothing. A faint scratching sound came from the direction of the door. Noni glanced up. Rosa and Alika made no sign that they'd heard anything. They were both absorbed in their own thoughts. Noni put down her needle and studied the wrinkles on her mother's forehead, her brother's scars, her own leg, lying propped up against a chair, all the way across the room from her. She thought about all the things they had lost, the ways they had all been marked. But she saw now that they had barely been touched. Not before this.

"What's that noise?" Rosa asked.

"What noise?"

"That. Listen."

They all listened. A faint sound, like a delicate moaning, wavered thinly into the room. It stopped. Then the scratching began again, a soft rasp, like the steady scraping of fingernails on sandpaper.

Noni shivered. If Rosa and Alika could hear the noise, too... She strapped on her leg and walked out of the kitchen. She opened the back door and stepped onto the porch. There she saw the source of the noise. Alika had forgotten to bring Wendy's kite inside. It was leaning up against the side of the house, under the window, scraping against the stucco with every gust of wind.

Noni took the kite inside and propped it against the wall beside the back door. She returned to the kitchen, where Alika and Rosa waited.

"It's just the wind," she said.

And then the telephone rang.

—

What I'd wanted was drama, the astonished release of suspense, crescendo, an ending that would crack the air like lightning after a humid day.

But it was all very quiet. Just before I came back, I saw the whole continent spread out below me; my vision widened until I could see the Arctic regions and the Gulf of Mexico, the Atlantic, the Pacific, and even Hawaii, way off to the side.

I saw the waters of the Red River flowing all the way up from the Mississippi, pouring into Lake Winnipeg and then the Churchill River, emptying into Hudson's Bay. And from the west, the wide Assiniboine, snaking south and north and south again, through the foothills of the Riding Mountain and the plains of Manitoba.

In all that space, all that vast continent, you'd think those two rivers could manage to avoid each other, but somehow they couldn't. They ran smack into each other. They coincided. Here. In the city where I was born and had died. And I thought that if such a thing could happen, such an unlikely event, then nearly any accidental meeting might be possible here. Even mine and Marty Smith's. Because this was a place of unlikely events. The exact, geographical centre of coincidence.

AGMV Marquis

MEMBER OF SCABRINI MEDIA

Quebec, Canada
2002